Mystery and Confidence

A Tale.
Volume. 1

Elizabeth Sibthorpe Pinchard

Alpha Editions

This edition published in 2024

ISBN : 9789361479571

Design and Setting By
Alpha Editions
www.alphaedis.com
Email - info@alphaedis.com

Contents

CHAP. I.

Due westward, fronting to the green,
A rural portico was seen,
Where Ellen's hand had taught to twine
The ivy and Idean vine;
The clematis, the favor'd flow'r,
Which boasts the name of virgin's bow'r.

LADY OF THE LAKE.

At the foot of one of the most romantic mountains in North Wales, about a mile from the coast of Carnarvonshire, stands the little village of Llanwyllan: there, amongst trees which seemed coeval with the dwelling, was a very large farm-house, the residence of Farmer Powis. Its high chimneys, and neatly white-washed walls, rendered it a pleasing object to those who travelled on the high-road, about a mile off, which led to the next market-town, if high-road that might be called which merely served to facilitate the journies of the neighbouring farmers' wives to market and back again, or those of the curate, who served the churches in the immediate vicinity. The hand of native taste had removed a few branches from the immense trees which shaded this rural dwelling, and by that means afforded to the inhabitants a view of the road, the spire of the village church, and two or three natural rills of water, which, falling from the adjacent hills, increased the beauty of the scene. At this dwelling a traveller arrived on the evening of a day which had been intensely hot, in the summer of 18—: the dust which covered his shoes, and almost concealed the colour of his coat, declared him a pedestrian; probably, therefore, of inferior rank; yet, under the shade which fatigue had thrown over his features, might be discerned a fine and interesting countenance; and when at the door of the farm-house, where Powis sat inhaling the mixed fumes of his evening pipe, and the fragrance of a fine honeysuckle which entwined around the porch, he inquired the nearest way to——, the tones of his voice, and the fineness of his accent, would, to a practised ear, have proclaimed a man who had mixed with the higher orders of society: to Powis, however, they conveyed no idea but that the traveller was weary and spoke with civility; and either would have demanded from him civility, nay, kindness in return: he rose therefore from his seat, and pushing aside his little table, made room for the stranger, and requested him to be seated. The stranger thankfully complied, and taking off his hat, wiped the dust from his face, and shewed a fine forehead and eyes, whose brilliant rays seemed more obscured by sorrow than by time, though he appeared to be about five-and-thirty. While the farmer went into the house to order some refreshment for his weary guest, the stranger turned his eyes, and saw with surprise that every thing about him bore the marks of taste; of taste not indeed highly refined, but simple, natural, and delicate: every tree round the spot on which he sat was intertwined with woodbines, clematis, and the wild hop; and the long shoots of all were carried from tree to tree, forming festoons of exquisite grace and beauty. At the foot of each tree a space had been cleared and filled with fragrant plants, whose culture requires little trouble. Mignionette, roses, pinks, and carnations, perfumed the air, while the too powerful seringa was only suffered to rise at a considerable distance, whence its odour came occasionally wafted by the evening breeze, and (if the expression may be allowed) harmonized well with the softer scents in the immediate vicinity of the dwelling. A variety of birds in the adjacent orchard and fields yet poured their mingled songs, which, as the sun declined gradually, sunk into a softer strain, and soon all was hushed into repose. In the meantime the table was spread with a neat cloth, cold meat, brown bread, some fresh-gathered fruit, cream, ale, and home-made wine; each excellent in its kind.

The farmer had not asked his guest to "*take some refreshment,*" the phrase being probably unknown to him, but with genuine hospitality, seeing he was fatigued, concluded it would be acceptable, and pressed him to partake of what was set before them; then calling to the servant girl, who had spread the table, he said something to her in Welsh, which she answered in the same language. "That is unlucky," said Powis: "my daughter, Sir, is absent just now; she is gone to the curate's, the only house in the neighbourhood she likes to visit at; indeed, she has reason to like it, for Mrs. Ross has taught Ellen to sew and to read, and be a tolerable housewife, ever since my poor wife died, which happened when Ellen was a little child; and she looks upon Mrs. Ross as her mother, and Joanna Ross, who is nearly her own age, as her sister: they are good companions for each other, and good girls both, I assure you: however, we will not wait, for perhaps Ellen may not be at home this half hour or more." "I fear," said the stranger, "I have induced you to hasten your meal, and perhaps——" "Not at all, not at all," interrupted Powis. "Ellen can eat her fruit and milk at any time, or perhaps will partake of our good parson's supper; never mind her." "You are indeed very kind; but I fear it grows late. How far have I to walk to the little inn where you said I might procure a bed?" "About half a mile: but the moon is rising, and one of my boys shall shew you the way: you may be sure of a bed; they have two to spare; both clean and decent, though plain and homely; and we have few travellers in these parts."

Some more conversation passed, and then, the stranger having eaten as much as he liked, and withstood an earnest solicitation to eat a great deal more, rose to depart. The boy was called, and the charge given to him in Welsh to recommend the stranger to the best attentions of neighbour Jones, at the sign of the Prince of Wales; being explained to the traveller in English, he took his leave.

In the course of the conversation which passed between them, the stranger told Powis that he was travelling merely for amusement, and preferred walking to any other mode of conveyance, as affording him better opportunities of exploring the romantic scenery with which Wales abounds; but this the farmer imagined was the language of a man, who, although he was poor, did not wish to be thought so. He said he was so much pleased with what he had seen of the country round Llanwyllan, that it was his intention to remain there a few days, if he found tolerable accommodations at the inn; and Powis gave him a pressing invitation to rest whenever he pleased at his house, and to partake of his dinner or supper; for in that retired spot, where fraud and deceit were almost unknown, suspicion was equally a stranger, nor arose to check that frank hospitality man should naturally afford to man. The stranger said he had left his portmanteau at Carnarvon, and should send a man to fetch it the next day, if he determined on remaining at the village. Powis mentioned several points of view which he said were thought fine, though he professed not to understand the business much.

As the stranger, with his little Welsh guide, passed through the trees which grew round the house, just where the shadow was deepest, he discerned the flutter of the white or light-coloured garments of two girls, and heard youthful voices in chat, and laughing; yet not rudely or with vulgarity, but with native gaiety and mirth of heart. He could just distinguish that one of the females was taller than the other, and heard a soft harmonious voice articulate in good English, and with very little of the Welsh accent: "Good night, dear Joanna; come to-morrow, and stay with me all day: good night; love to Charles." The other replied at a few paces distant: "Ah, poor Charles! how vexed he will be that he staid so late; well, good night, Ellen."

"These, I suppose," thought the stranger, "are Powis's daughter and her friend Joanna Ross. I am glad I missed them. I hate country-girls. Charles I imagine is the lover of one. Happy creatures who can yet fancy felicity in love, and dream I know not what of constancy and bliss!—Falsehood, jealousy, revenge!—dreadful, dreadful words! to them are unknown: but what have I to do with thoughts like these? Why, even in the stillness of this calm retreat, do such shocking images haunt my mind?" He hurried on as if fatigue had no longer power over him, insomuch that his young guide could hardly keep up with him, till he reached the village inn, where, as Powis had said, a cleanly though homely bed was soon prepared for him.

CHAP. II.

Her form was fresher than the morning rose,
When the dew wets its leaves, unstain'd and pure
As is the lily, or the mountain snow.
The modest virtues mingled in her eyes.

THOMSON.

In the evening of the next day, having in the course of it received his portmanteau from Carnarvon, our traveller, whose name he gave his landlord to understand was Mordaunt, began slowly to ascend a romantic mountain, stopping at intervals to admire the beauty of the surrounding prospect, and occasionally selecting from the mountain plants such specimens as he had not met with before; for our traveller was an excellent botanist, had a slight knowledge of mineralogy, and a genuine taste for the charms of nature. In what farther sciences he was instructed, and how he came by information so much above his present sphere, we shall learn as we proceed.

Mordaunt had wandered more than an hour, when he reached some slight remains of an ancient castle: it was a complete ruin, affording no shelter, and scarcely a resting-place; however, on a large stone, which had fallen from one of the crumbling pillars, he sat down and enjoyed the beauty of the extensive prospect before him, and to which no descriptive powers short of Mrs. Radcliffe's could do justice: here he remained, catching, at intervals, a distant sail; for the sea, not far off, formed one magnificent feature in the view; till the shades of evening appeared to close upon him somewhat suddenly: surprised at the gloom, he turned round, and observed that the top of the mountain behind him was covered with heavy clouds, which soon becoming thicker, fell around him in large drops of rain, mingled with low muttering thunder, and distant gleams of lightning: the sea assumed a more terrific appearance, and the lashing of the waves against the shore was more distinctly heard: every thing, in short, seemed to foretell a tremendous storm.

The gloomy woods
Start at the flash, and from their deep recess,
Wide flaming out their trembling inmates shake!
Amid Carnarvon's mountains rages loud
The repercussive roar; with mighty crush,
Into the flashing deep from the rude rocks
Of Penmanmawr heap'd hideous to the sky,

Tumble the smitten cliffs; and Snowden's peak,
Dissolving, instant yields his wintry load.

THOMSON.

Yet Mordaunt, unappall'd, was rather pleased to have an opportunity of observing the effects of a thunder-storm in a region so elevated; but in a moment, a vivid flash of lightning, followed instantly by a tremendous burst of thunder, was succeeded by a piercing scream; and two girls, descending the mountain, ran by him with the utmost swiftness. The rain, which now fell in torrents, had already wetted their slight garments, and as the descent was now become extremely slippery, one of them had nearly fallen to the ground, at the instant she had passed him. Humanity prompted Mordaunt to follow, entreat them not to be alarmed, and to allow him to assist them: his appearance, so totally unexpected (for the shadow of the ruin under which he stood, and the deep gloom of the atmosphere, had prevented their seeing him), seemed to startle them almost as much as the storm, which one of the half-breathless girls said had surprized them still higher on the mountain than he had been. The thunder, however, now became more distant; and a light breeze, springing up from the land, carried the clouds towards the sea: still, however, the descent continued dangerous, from being so slippery; and Mordaunt solicited the young women to accept of his aid. He readily conjectured them to be Joanna Ross and Ellen Powis; and the moment the soft voice of the latter fell upon his ear, he recognized the speaker he had heard the night before saying, "Good night, dear Joanna." Her voice, indeed, was so singularly sweet, that once heard it could never be forgotten; and Mordaunt, turning as she spoke, beheld a face and figure, which, once seen, must equally be for ever remembered—

And ne'er did Grecian chisel trace
A nymph, a Naïad, or a Grace,
Of finer form or lovelier face.
What though the sun, with ardent frown,
Had slightly ting'd her cheek with brown;
What though no rule of courtly grace
To measur'd mood had train'd her pace.
A foot more light, a step more true,
Ne'er from the heath-flow'r dash'd the dew:
E'en the slight hare-bell rais'd its head
Elastic from her airy tread.
What though upon her speech there hung
Some accents of the mountain tongue;

Those silver sounds, so soft, so dear,
The list'ner held his breath to hear.

SCOTT'S LADY OF THE LAKE

Terror had, indeed, robbed her charming countenance of some of its graces; but a bright blush, springing to her cheeks as she caught the traveller's glance, restored its native lustre. Oh! such a face!—so fair—so bright—so spotless!—eyes so full of soul!—a smile of such inimitable beauty! Every feature expressing a native delicacy of sentiment, unsoiled by the world, unruffled by passion, yet giving assurance that its possessor owned a heart of such fine frame as seldom can be met with, either in court or cottage. And when with sweet confidence, which, intending no harm, feared none, she accepted Mordaunt's offered arm, he felt a degree of pleasure to which he had long been a stranger: he scarcely noticed that Joanna had taken the other arm: yet Joanna was not a plain girl; but who could look at her when Ellen was present? As they descended the mountain, the storm having by this time blown over, the girls laughed at their vain terrors, and made light of those which Mordaunt expressed, lest their wet clothes should give them cold, saying, they were so accustomed to take exercise in all weathers, they were not likely to be injured by a sudden shower: "Though I must acknowledge," said Joanna, with a smile, "we do not much like thunder-storms." Every thing that either said was expressed in the plural; and "*We*" was always the term, whichever spoke. Mordaunt admired the good sense and propriety with which each seemed endowed; but in Ellen he distinguished an elegance of expression, a superiority of mind, which, in so young a girl, and one who could have had so few opportunities of improvement, completely surprised him. This lovely creature seemed yet hardly seventeen; and when he talked to her on various subjects, he found, that although Mr. Ross's library had furnished her with the works of Addison, Pope, and a few more of our best English authors, yet her acquisitions had not gone beyond a tincture of English literature, in a general way; that she was tolerably well instructed in English History, knew scarcely any thing of Geography, and could neither play on any instrument nor draw; so that she certainly was much inferior to the heroines of some modern novels, who learn all these things by intuition: her voice, however, in singing, was as harmonious as in speaking, and she could sing many of the simple Welsh airs with natural taste, and in a very pleasing manner. Mordaunt escorted the girls to Llanwyllan Farm, where he was immediately recognized by Powis, who, hearing from his daughter the attention he had shewn to her and Joanna, was cordial in his acknowledgments, and insisted on the traveller partaking their supper. Mordaunt could not refuse; and it was accordingly spread, not as usual in the porch, the late storm having left a dampness in the air, but in a large hall, the farm-house having formerly been a capital mansion.

Joanna and Ellen, having hastily changed their wet garments, soon joined them; and this little party sat down to supper pleased with each other, and without any of that cold formality which strangers so generally feel; confiding hospitality on the one hand, and something, at least, very like good breeding, on the other, rendering them all easy and pleasant to themselves, and to each other.

During this little repast, though no ill-timed curiosity demanded the explanation, Mordaunt thought proper to mention his name, and, in some degree, declare his situation in life. He had, he said, been educated with the Earl of St. Aubyn, who was his distant relation, and had a few years before appointed him his steward for his estate in Northamptonshire, where he had a comfortable house, not far from St. Aubyn Castle, the noble residence of the Earl himself, who had been for sometime on the Continent; that he himself, having met with some domestic vexations, which had injured his health, the Earl had permitted him to appoint a deputy, and travel into Wales, as he had done the summer before into the Highlands of Scotland; of which he gave a most animated description. His patron, he added, had also a fine estate on the borders of Westmoreland, with a very noble old seat called the Abbey, which, though extremely ancient, still retained its former magnificence. Mordaunt's manners were so pleasing, his voice so impressive, and his countenance so fine, that the little party who were his auditors hung upon his words with almost breathless admiration.—The moments flew, and they were surprised when the hall clock struck eleven, an hour unheard of among the sober inhabitants of Llanwyllan. "God bless me," said Powis, "why it's eleven o'clock: I have not been up so late these ten years!" "Dear father!" said Ellen, with a reproving accent, as she glanced at Mordaunt, who hastily rose from his chair. "Excuse my rudeness, Sir," said Powis; "I did not mean to turn you out uncivilly, but fear neighbour Jones may be gone to bed." Mordaunt smiled, and said he ought to apologize for keeping them up. Then extending his hand, he shook the farmer's rough one with great kindness, and said, "If I should not see you again——" "Not see us again!" interrupted Powis: "why to be sure you are not going away! Lord bless me— why, I thought you would stay a day or two at least; for my share, if you don't, I wish you had never come at all; for I never saw a man in all my days I liked so well." "Upon my word, Sir," said Joanna, "you have not yet seen half the beauties of Llanwyllan; has he, Ellen?" "No, indeed," replied Ellen. "I assure you, Mr. Mordaunt, there are many charms—" "I know it, I feel it!" interrupted Mordaunt: "there is every charm which the most beautiful nature, the kindest hospitality, can bestow! But to stay at the village without visiting the Farm of Llanwyllan would be impossible, and, stranger as I am, would it not be intruding?" "Not at all," said Powis; "we should rejoice to keep you amongst us; the girls will shew you the fine views, as they call them, and I shall be proud to see you at my table, if it be not too plain for you, at all times." "You are too good! but, will Miss Ross, will Miss Powis, accept their share of the agreement? Are there no more agreeable engagements, no more amiable friends to claim their attention?" He took a hand of each, but fixed his penetrating eyes on Ellen: she blushed, but the lightest emotion made Ellen blush, so that though Mordaunt had "*Charles*" in his head when he spoke, he could judge nothing by her blushing; and her eyes met his with a look of confiding sweetness, which seemed to speak a heart unconscious of any secret sentiment. Joanna answered, "If we were to tell you, Mr. Mordaunt, we had nothing to do but to walk about, you would think we were very idle girls, or said what was not true: we are very busy all the day till five in the evening, when we drink tea either here or at my father's, who will be happy to see you: after that, if it is fine we walk; if not, amuse ourselves within, till ten o'clock, when we go to bed, that we may rise at five the next morning; from five in the evening till ten we shall be glad of your company."

In consequence of this frank statement, and the secret inclination he felt to see more of Llanwyllan, and its art-less inhabitants, Mordaunt determined to pass a few days there; and the next day, after attending their early tea-table, walked two or three hours with Ellen and Joanna, equally delighted with Powis's kind hospitality, and the unsuspicious confidence of the two innocent girls, who, stranger as he was, saw nothing extraordinary or improper in allowing him a degree of friendly intimacy, which, in a situation of more publicity, he would hardly have attained under some weeks of acquaintance, even with the assistance of a proper introduction. Still more was he charmed with their affectionate manner towards each other, and the beauty of Ellen, as well as her unaffected simplicity, united with an extraordinary share of good sense and information beyond her apparent opportunities. When they parted in the evening, Joanna said, "To-morrow, you know, Ellen, Charles will pass at home; and as he goes away entirely the next day, I think we must not make any engagement for to-morrow." "Very true," said Ellen, in a low voice, and a slight shade passed over her expressive features; but whether it arose from regret that she must relinquish the society of her new friend, with whose spirited and sensible conversation she appeared much pleased, or from concern for Charles's approaching absence, our traveller had no means of judging. He had discovered, in the course of conversation, that Charles was Joanna's brother, and was now absent for a day or two preparatory to his leaving home for some time, being in the navy: a few more particulars relative to him he felt anxious to ascertain as soon as possible; and he took leave of his new friends, after engaging to spend the next evening but one at Mr. Ross's.

The landlord at the Prince of Wales understood and spoke English; but it was with so much of the Welsh accent, that Mordaunt, with difficulty, comprehended his meaning. The curiosity which he felt, however, to learn more about Charles Ross, induced him, once again, to attempt a conversation with "neighbour Jones," as Powis called him, though, in general, Mordaunt's patience, which was by no means inexhaustible, and an ear refined by living much in his early days with people of fashion and learning, were severely tried by provincial dialects, and he avoided, as much as possible, any conference with those who spoke what he termed a barbarous jargon: for humour of any kind, or odd characters, whether natural or acquired, he had no taste; sentiment, elegance, and refinement of language and manners, were to him indispensable requisites of those be regarded; and above all things he detested that mixture of familiarity and obsequiousness which the landlord of a country inn shews to one, who, though his guest, he fancies his equal; yet there was some paramount feeling in Mordaunt's mind, which forced him to dispense with all these niceties, and seek intelligence even from a man whose language and manner were equally distasteful to him. From Jones, then, he learnt that Charles was the son of Mr. Ross, and that he was a young man of about twenty, rather handsome, a midshipman in the navy, and that he was going to join his ship immediately. Jones allowed that the general opinion was that Ellen Powis was the object of Charles's affections, and that all their friends wished it might be a match, but that Winifred Powis's old servant declared Miss Ellen only regarded him as a brother, and she was sure had no thought of being his wife. Mordaunt recollected the blush, the slight shade of gravity or vexation which had passed over Ellen's lovely face; yet these might not be symptoms of more than sisterly affection, and something whispered a wish to Mordaunt that Ellen's love for Charles might be no more.

Though Mordaunt could not intrude upon a party from which he had been by Joanna almost expressly interdicted, he yet, in returning from his ramble the next evening, contrived to pass the Parsonage, and to catch a glimpse of Ellen and Joanna walking in the garden with a young man. He bowed to them, and saw that their companion, whom he naturally concluded was Charles, took some hasty steps from the path he was walking in, to catch a nearer view of him; and Mordaunt fancied, from the earnestness of his gestures, and something of impatience in his air, when he rejoined his sister and her friend, that he spoke of him, and with displeasure: perhaps he was jealous of his attentions towards Ellen.—"Well, be it so," said Mordaunt; "I shall soon discover if he has any influence over her mind; and if I perceive that she wishes my absence, I will immediately quit Llanwyllan. Not for worlds would I make that lovely creature unhappy; far otherwise. If there be any engagement between her and this fortunate Charles, I will do all I can to promote his interest: but if, on the other hand, I find her to-morrow only lamenting him as a friend, I will yet linger here awhile, and forget, if possible, in this sweet retirement, and her enchanting society, *all the past*! Oh that I could as easily forget all the future threatens! Happy, most happy, could I here remain for ever! That, alas! cannot, must not be! Edmund, cruel, vindictive Edmund!—Ah! those dark eyes pursue me every where: in the gloom of night they are before me, demanding vengeance—vengeance for her blood! speaking volumes of hatred—of revenge! What a fate is mine! Soon, too soon, we must meet again!" Thus murmured Mordaunt, in one of those soliloquies to which he had accustomed himself; and his pace, sometimes fast, sometimes slow, betrayed the agitation of his mind. At length he came within sight of Llanwyllan Farm; and leaning on the little green gate which led to the house, the mixed odours of those sweet plants, which he now knew were Ellen's care, struck upon his senses: her lovely image rose renewed to his imagination, and the distant water-fall and rising moon seemed combined with that enchanting scent to lull his anguish to repose. Whilst he yet lingered, he saw through the trees Ellen, Joanna, and Charles, approaching; and Mordaunt hastily retired, with sensations not very unlike indignation and envy.

CHAP. III.

When he speaks,
The air, a charter'd libertine, is still,
And the mute wonder lurketh in mens' ears,
To steal his sweet and honey'd sentences!

HENRY V.

The following evening, when Mordaunt arrived at the Parsonage, he was met in the little garden before it by Joanna and Ellen. He glanced his eyes over the countenances of both, and found that of Joanna, which he had hitherto seen full of smiling vivacity, overspread with gloom: her eyes were excessively red, and when he spoke to her, they filled with tears. Ellen also looked as if she had been weeping, but on Mordaunt's approach, a bright smile gleamed over her face, and a soft blush restored its animation.

As Mordaunt looked inquiringly at Joanna (dissembling as well as he could the pleasure Ellen's blush and smile had given him), she turned her head aside, and the tears ran down her cheeks: "Don't look at her, don't speak to her, Mr. Mordaunt," said Ellen in a low voice, drawing him a little on one side: "her brother has left home this morning, and Joanna has been crying all day." Her voice trembled, and a tear started in her own eye. Mordaunt softly drew her arm through his; and as Joanna turned into another walk to hide her distress, he said, "And you too, Ellen, have been weeping." He had never called her Ellen before, and felt half ashamed of having done so now, so much respect her native modesty had inspired; but she, who was always accustomed to be called Ellen, nor imagined she had any pretension to a higher title, saw nothing in it extraordinary, and answered in the most unaffected manner, yet with some tenderness of voice and accent, "It is very true, I also feel for Charles a sister's affection." "Is he then *very* amiable, this happy Charles?" asked Mordaunt. "He is very amiable, that is, very *good*, very *sensible*," said Ellen: "but why do you call him happy?"—"Can he be otherwise than happy, rich in the affection of *two* such charming *sisters*?" "You are very obliging but just now Charles is not very happy; he is very much grieved at quitting his father, his mother, and Joanna, and—and—me." Ellen hesitated a little. "But in the profession he has chosen," said Mordaunt, "he must expect to be frequently absent from those he loves; and a sailor in general, though he feels acutely for the moment, soon whistles care away." "Very true," answered Ellen; "and I never before knew Charles give way to his feelings as he has done to-day and yesterday, and that indeed is what has overcome Joanna so much: he has taken strange fancies into his head, either that he shall never return, or that *we*, I mean that *I*, shall have forgotten him if he does." "But why does he fancy this *just now*?" said Mordaunt, fixing his sparkling eyes upon her. "Oh, I cannot tell you," answered Ellen, blushing crimson, "half the strange things he has been saying; but we see so few strangers here, that I believe, that I fancy Charles supposes,—I mean, he thinks we have suddenly become very intimate with *you*, and we have said so much respecting books and subjects rather above what we usually meet with, that Charles, who is a little rough, and not very fond of reading, says we are growing such fine ladies, and so much wiser than he is, that he is sure we shall not be at all sorry he is going."

Mordaunt paused a moment. One of the reflections of the preceding night passed through his mind—what was he doing? was he making this amiable young creature unhappy? was he sowing discord between her and a young man to whom she was perhaps attached, and who certainly was so to her? and, after all, to what purpose? He continued silent so long, that the innocent Ellen, looking in his face, and seeing his countenance discomposed, hastily said, "Pray, Mr. Mordaunt, do not be offended. Charles is naturally kind and hospitable, and I am sure would blush for us if we were not attentive to a stranger whose behaviour has been so obliging to us; but just now his temper is ruffled, and he certainly has said a great many odd things lately." "Offended I can have no right to be," answered Mordaunt; "but if I give offence by staying here, Miss Powis, either to you or *your friends*, I shall indeed be sorry that I did not, as I at first intended, leave Llanwyllan yesterday." "Pray do not suppose it. I cannot tell why I repeated all these silly things to you, but I am so apt to speak all I think, and so unused to form and ceremony, that I dare say I must appear very strange to you, who have lived so much in the world. I begin *now* to wish what I never wished before." "What is that, Ellen?" "That I also had lived more in the world, that my manners might have been a little more polished, and not so—so—strange as I must seem to *you*." "Artless and ever amiable creature!" exclaimed Mordaunt with a vehemence which almost made her start: "what, oh, what could the world have done for you! Believe me, Ellen, for one grace it could have given, it would have robbed you of a thousand."

At this moment, when Mordaunt, startled by his own warmth, wished to have recalled his words, when Ellen became so confused by it, she could make no answer, Joanna rejoined them, and asked him if he would not walk in, saying her father and mother were waiting for them. "Indeed, Miss Ross," said Mordaunt, "I think I have done wrong in coming hither to-day. Your parents, distrest by parting from their son, should not be broken in upon by a stranger." "Pray do not judge of them by my folly," answered Joanna: "they have parted from Charles before: as his absence will probably not exceed a few months, they are now quite composed, and will be glad to see you."

Joanna led the way to a very neat little parlour, where Mr. and Mrs. Ross, with the tea-table placed before the latter, were waiting to receive them. Mr. Ross was a man far advanced in life, who in the early part of it had been accustomed to genteel society, was an excellent classical scholar, and well grounded in English literature of a superior class, as well as what is properly termed the Belles Lettres. He had greatly ameliorated the condition of his parishioners, by introducing industry and neatness in their habitations, yet he had merely tinctured the minds of Ellen and Joanna with a love of reading, justly conceiving that in their station of life much literary knowledge and refinement of taste would be worse than useless to them. The gay heart of Joanna had been well content to skim the mere surface; but Ellen, more serious, and with more native delicacy of taste, had often excited the anger of Mrs. Ross by the reluctance with which she left her studies, and tore herself from the polished pages of Addison and Pope, to sit down to heavy needlework, or make preserves. Every thing worthy of observation which Ellen heard or read she made her own, not only by the aid of memory, but by that happy nameless faculty which selects the best of every thing, and combining ideas with admirable facility, extracts knowledge and wit from what to common minds presents little better than an uninteresting blank. An old magazine in Ellen's hands became a commentary on the history of the times to which it belonged; and while other girls would have been idling over the tales, or puzzling themselves with the enigmas, it contained, she was selecting and classing a store of facts and characteristic anecdotes, which, with a very little assistance, would have been a foundation for the most accurate historical knowledge: thus, like the bee, from the most unpromising materials, Ellen extracted the honey, and left the refuse behind. In this manner, and with the aid of very few books, she had obtained a degree of information, which many women, whose educations are most anxiously attended to, never attain. Another circumstance was, that having no great variety of authors, she was obliged to repeat the perusal of those she was allowed to read, and by that means had time thoroughly to digest and comprehend them; whereas, the young people of the present day have such an endless variety of books offered to them, that nothing which has not the charm of novelty can be endured, and scarcely any merit can obtain a second reading.

Mrs. Ross was a little, bustling, notable woman, who picqued herself upon her good housewifery, could not endure a *litter*, and thought books and papers made the most intolerable of any: Mr. Ross was therefore obliged to confine his to his study, and the girls the few they were allowed to their own bed-room, which was considered equally the apartment of Ellen and Joanna. Mr. Ross had heard a great deal for the last two or three days of Mr. Mordaunt from his daughter and Ellen: he saw they were greatly pleased with their new acquaintance; but knowing their simplicity, and the charm of novelty to youth, was desirous of judging for himself how far the traveller was a proper companion for them. Ross had formerly seen something of the world, and was of course more qualified to judge of character than Powis, or two girls so totally unacquainted with guile as Ellen and Joanna were: he determined, if he found any thing in the manners of the stranger repulsive to his ideas of propriety, to put an end to all connection with him; and Mrs. Ross, who felt assured the traveller must have fallen in love with one of the girls, resolved, as she expressed it, to keep a *sharp look out* upon him: such, however, was the unaffected propriety of Mordaunt's manners, mingled with somewhat of dignity, to which Mrs. Ross had never been accustomed, and which Ross had not lately seen, that the good little woman was awed into silence; and though Charles had infected her with some of his jealous fears (for such they certainly were), she soon lost the kind of prejudice she had taken up against the traveller, was pleased with "*the gentleman*," as she called him, and could not ascertain at all to her own satisfaction whether Joanna or Ellen, or either, had been his inducement to remain at Llanwyllan.

Ross was not only charmed with Mordaunt's manners, but had not for years enjoyed so exquisite a treat as his conversation. The traveller was fully competent to cope even with Ross on literary ground, understood the learned languages, was an enthusiast in the classics, an excellent historian and geographer; and gave Ross in an hour the most perspicuous account of all that was then passing in the political world.

The two girls sat attentive auditors: Ellen seemed all ear. Mrs. Ross at last began to fidget a little, and soon after walked off to superintend some domestic concerns, but, unusually indulgent, suffered the girls to remain. The evening passed on, and Ross was so engaged with his guest, that walking could not be proposed. Mordaunt expressed himself so charmed with Llanwyllan, that he said, if he could be accommodated with a neat lodging, he should after about a fortnight's absence, which was absolutely necessary, endeavour to obtain Lord St. Aubyn's consent to an arrangement, which might permit him to remain there some time; that he found the pure air from the mountains agreed with him, and thought two or three months, divested of the cares of business, in that peaceful retirement, would quite restore his health. Ross knew that if Powis heard his proposal, he would, in the warmth and cordiality of his heart, offer Mordaunt apartments at Llanwyllan Farm, where indeed there was plenty of room; but Ross also knew, though Powis did not, that apartments under the same room with such a lovely girl as Ellen Powis, for a man not passed the meridian of life, would be highly improper, and even in that retired place would subject Ellen to unpleasant remarks; he therefore immediately said that there were two neat quiet rooms at the house of a widow in the village, who, having lately lost her son, would be glad to let them; that she was a very civil old woman, and had formerly been cook in a gentleman's family; and though the rooms might not be furnished quite well enough for Mr. Mordaunt, yet any little accommodation might easily be added at an inconsiderable expense from Carnarvon, which was not more than twelve miles from Llanwyllan. Mordaunt eagerly caught at the proposal, and said that a few guineas, when compared to the recovery of his health, were not material to him; it was therefore settled that he should go with Ross the next day to look at the rooms. Mordaunt then rose to take leave, but the entrance of Mrs. Ross, followed by the servant with a couple of hot roasted chickens, &c. prevented him, and an earnest invitation to stay and partake of their supper, which indeed seemed to have been greatly enlarged on his account, could not be resisted. Mordaunt of course complied: the conversation became more general: Mrs. Ross's tarts, home-made wines, &c. were excellent, and Mordaunt praised them too much not to become a favourite with the good lady. He sat by Ellen, and a few words spoken to her occasionally in a low voice, and, still more, the expressive manner in which they were said, began to raise suspicions in Ross's mind that she was in reality the magnet which attracted the stranger. He was not blind to her superior beauty and native elegance, and considered her as more peculiarly his care, inasmuch as he knew the guileless simplicity of Powis, and that he was by no means calculated to have the guidance of so lovely a girl. Ross determined therefore to watch carefully over Ellen, and if he saw any thing too particular in Mordaunt's conduct towards her, to advise Powis to send her from home during the traveller's stay at Llanwyllan, which, as Powis had a relation at Bangor, would be very possible. Ellen was to sleep that night at the Parsonage; and as soon as Mordaunt took his leave, the two girls retired together.

Ellen was so silent, that Joanna began to rally her on the subject of the stranger, and amongst other things said, "Indeed, Ellen, I believe poor Charles was right. Mr. Mordaunt will soon take his place in your affections." "*His* place, *Charles's* place! no, indeed, Joanna!" "Well, you may say what you please, Ellen; but Charles never gained half so much attention from you as you bestowed on Mr. Mordaunt's conversation to-night"—"Perhaps not: Charles never conversed on such agreeable topics." "Then why do you say you do not, nor shall, like him so well as you do Charles?" "I did not say so." "Well, but you said he would not take Charles's place in your affections, and that is the same thing." "Nor will he. I love Charles as a brother, you as a sister; but does it follow no other man or woman can be agreeable to me— must I cease to love you both before I can be pleased with another?" "No, certainly; but Charles I am persuaded would not much relish such a degree of liking for another, as Mordaunt seems to have gained from you." "I cannot help that: I shall never think myself obliged to consult Charles respecting my likings or dislikings." "What, not if you marry him?" "Marry Charles!"—"Aye, *marry Charles*, Miss Powis: what is there so wonderful in that?" "Dear Joanna,

I do not know you to-night. *Miss Powis!* and in that reproachful tone: what have I done to offend you, and why do you call me *Miss Powis?*" "Then why do you seem so surprised at the idea of marrying Charles, and look as if you quite scorned the thought?" "Because such an idea never entered my mind: I might well therefore seem surprised; though, as to scorn, I never felt or could have looked it." "If Mordaunt had said half as much to you as Charles has, you would easily have seen *his* meaning." "You are not kind, Joanna. I thought you had liked Mordaunt too." "So I do; but I do not like that he should prevent Charles from gaining your love." "Then, be assured, that cannot be: I love Charles as a brother, but if I had never seen Mordaunt, or any other man, I would not have been Charles's wife. Mordaunt does not, cannot think any thing of me: and I hope, Joanna, I am not such a bold girl as to fall in love, as they call it, with a man who will not, I am sure, ever cast a serious thought on *me*, who is so very much above me." "Then why do you declare so seriously against Charles: you never did so before?" "Because you never pressed me so earnestly before, and I assure you I never thought of it." "But what are your objections to Charles as a husband?" "Many, Joanna, many: he is too hasty, too passionate: he would frighten me." "And how do you know Mordaunt is not passionate?" "Still Mordaunt!" said Ellen, a little impatiently: "what signifies to me whether he is passionate or not? He will never be more to me than an agreeable acquaintance,"—"Well, I think Mordaunt has at times an odd look with his eyes, and a gloom on his countenance that is frightful." "Frightful! Mordaunt's countenance frightful! I never saw any thing so handsome; and the expression is the softest—his smile the sweetest—" Ellen paused with some embarrassment, and Joanna answered a little spitefully, "That may be, when he looks at *you*; and then you blush, and cast down your eyes, and of course do not see how *he* looks; but I tell you that he *has* a gloom that is *frightful*, though you are so astonished at the word, and so delighted with him." Here the shrill voice of Mrs. Ross calling to them from her own room, "Girls, girls, do you mean to talk all night," put an end to the conference, and they hastily said "Good night," less pleased with each other than they had ever been before. Joanna was angry with Ellen for preferring Mordaunt to Charles, and Ellen thought Joanna extremely captious, and out of humour.

The next day, Mordaunt, accompanied by Mr. Ross, looked at the lodgings he had proposed for him, and agreed immediately to take them for three months, to commence at the expiration of three weeks from the present time, during which, he said, he must take a journey to Bath, where he should see Lord St. Aubyn, and obtain his consent to an arrangement which would admit of his leaving Northamptonshire for that time; and that during his absence from Llanwyllan he should send some books and other additional comforts to his new lodgings: he should set out, he said, the next day but one, for he was impatient to begin his journey, that he might return the sooner. On the intermediate day, he walked to the Farm, and, strange to tell, found Ellen without Joanna.

Ellen had been very busy all day, and a little coldness still hung about Joanna, who could not forget her decided rejection of Charles: she had also been much employed, and told Ellen the evening before she should not see her on that day. "But Mr. Mordaunt will," added she, with some asperity, "and that will make full amends for my absence." "You are unkind, Joanna," answered Ellen, "and will make me wish Mr. Mordaunt had never visited Llanwyllan." Joanna shook her head with an air of incredulity, and left her. Mordaunt found Ellen therefore alone, and busily engaged amongst her shrubs and flowers. The brisk evening air, exercise, and the delight she took in her employment, had given fresh beauty to her complexion, and new animation to her eyes. After the first greetings had passed, he requested to assist her, and mounting a ladder, which a Welsh boy, who was executing the more laborious parts of the employment held for him, he busied himself in giving a new turn to the festoons which hung from tree to tree. Ellen stood below, and as she looked up to direct him, a long shoot of the clematis fell from his hand, and became entangled in her straw hat. Fearing to break it, he descended, and while he endeavoured to untwist it, the straw hat fell to the ground; and as Ellen had not, as usual, her modest muslin cap, her beautiful hair became for the first time exposed to his view, and he stood gazing at her bright auburn ringlets and fair-polished temples, as if transfixed. Beautiful as he had always thought her, he never saw her look so beautiful as now, and her increasing colour at length reminded him that his gaze was becoming oppressive. Instantly he withdrew his eyes, and taking up the hat, and brushing off some dust which adhered to it, he presented it to her with an air of respect, and said, "I am a very awkward gardener; I have spoiled your bonnet." "Indeed," said Ellen, "on the contrary, I should think you had practised it all your life, you seem so well versed in the employment."— "Would to heaven I had," answered Mordaunt, "and never known any thing beyond the culture of these shrubs, and the sweet shades of Llanwyllan." And now Ellen saw for the first time a peculiar expression in his eyes, and a gloom over his countenance, which reminded her of what Joanna had said respecting him; but Ellen put a different construction upon it, and had she known Shakespeare would have said, "He wrings at some distress: would I might free it, what-e'er it be."

To divert his thoughts, she said, in the softest tone, "What a wish! How different are my sentiments! I would give worlds, had my lot resembled your's; had I been employed not solely in the culture of these trees, myself almost as much a vegetable, but, like you, cultivating my mind, my manners, and forming myself into a companion for—the wise and good!" The soft expressive pause spoke volumes to the heart of Mordaunt, and he could not help replying, "You are already a fit companion for angels."

A long pause ensued. Ellen again began her pleasant labours, and Mordaunt, with fresh eagerness, assisted her. At length he said, "When I come back, Ellen, will you permit me to recommend to your perusal some books, which I shall send to my lodgings?" "Ah," said Ellen, "with delight should I peruse them, but Mrs. Ross is so strict, she will not allow me to read at all, if she can help it; and my father expects me to obey her in every respect." "But surely Mr. Ross, who is so literary himself, would willingly indulge such a mind as your's, which so eagerly aspires to superior attainments." "Ah, no; Mr. Ross thinks that in our station any extraordinary refinement would be injurious, and only tend to make us discontented." "Those common-place ideas may do very well for Joanna Ross, and girls of common minds; but you, surely, ought to be guided by other maxims. Talents like your's demand cultivation so imperiously, it is a real cruelty to deny it." "Ah, Mr. Mordaunt, do not talk to me in this manner; I am enough inclined to lament the lowness of my condition; not from ambition, but from a desire of knowledge, which, circumstanced as I am, is quite out of my reach. Rather strive to strengthen my mind, and my anxious wish to do my duty in the station where God has been pleased to place me." "Abhor me, Ellen, if ever you find me endeavouring to subvert one good and useful principle in your spotless mind; but how is Mr. Ross to know what station you may hereafter be called upon to fill, unless, indeed," added Mordaunt, expressively, "*your lot is already determined?*" "Undoubtedly it is," said Ellen (not understanding his allusion to Charles): "what can I have to expect but to remain here, the useful assistant of my father?" "But you may, nay, most probably will marry." "It is unlikely," said Ellen; "but if I should, it will probably be in a line of life which will render any farther literary attainments at best unprofitable; so at least says Mr. Ross, and I look to him as my chief director." "You have hitherto done well in so doing; but circumstances may hereafter arise to alter your views. In the meantime, let me assure you, for the honour of literature, that its female professors do not necessarily, according to a vulgar prejudice, become useless as mothers, mistresses, or domestic economists. I have actually seen a lady high not only in literary knowledge, but in literary fame, who attends with the most exquisite skill and propriety, not only to the management of a large family, but of a large farm, and whose order, neatness, and regularity, can no where be exceeded; yet this excellent woman has published many books, written in a style free from blemish, and full of the purest principles, and of the most superior good sense." "How well she must have arranged her concerns, and managed her time!" "Undoubtedly—and we shall see whether Ellen Powis has not mind enough to become a second Mrs. W——."

At this part of the conversation Powis joined them; and Mordaunt, having chatted a few minutes with him, took his leave. But though he had talked of leaving Llanwyllan on the next day, he did not go until that following; and on the Sunday he attended Mrs. Ross and the young people to the neat parish church, where he was greatly pleased and edified with the serious and dignified manner in which the venerable Ross performed the service. His fine countenance, shaded with grey hair, the rich tones of his voice, and the energetic manner in which he exhorted his rustic congregation, inspired Mordaunt with the utmost respect for him, and with a fervour of devotion he had rarely before experienced. Nor did he less admire the unaffected piety and attention of Mrs. Ross and her two pupils, who, once within the church, appeared too deeply impressed with the intention of their coming, to permit that either look or thought should stray to any other object. As they returned through the church-yard, Mordaunt was delighted to see the neatness, and even elegance with which this repository of the dead was kept. The graves, bound with osier-bands, and decorated with fresh flowers, as is customary through all Wales, excited in him sentiments of the tenderest nature; he was charmed to witness the effects of a love which survived the tomb, and whispered to Ellen, that wherever he lived, he should wish to be buried in Wales. "Idle as it may seem," said he, "to care what becomes of this perishable frame when the immortal spirit is fled, yet in the truth of Gray's inimitable reflections on this subject I cannot but coincide:—

"Even from the grave the voice of Nature cries,
Even in our ashes live their wonted fires."

As Ellen had never met with Gray, Mordaunt now repeated to her some of the finest stanzas, and promised to send her the poem in the morning following.

What a happiness for her that she had never been condemned to hear this enchanting elegy hacknied till even its beauties are lost in the insipid recitation of girls who learn it as a task.

CHAP. IV.

A prattling gossip, on whose tongue
Proof of perpetual motion hung,
Who with a hundred pair of eyes,
The vain attacks of sleep defies;
Who with a hundred pair of wings,
News from the farthest quarters brings,
Sees, hears, and tells, untold before,
All that she knows, and ten times more.

CHURCHILL.

When Mordaunt was gone, Joanna and Ellen returned to their usual manner of living: at first Ellen found a great insipidity in her ordinary occupations. The day seemed unusually tedious, but this by degrees wore off; and had she never seen Mordaunt again, she would certainly have always remembered him with peculiar interest; but the peace of her mind was undisturbed: yet Mordaunt's conversation had been of the most dangerous tendency. What girl of seventeen, tinctured with the natural romance which a life in a country of such sublimity as Wales almost necessarily produces in an ardent mind and feeling heart, but might be led by the voice of flattery to believe herself superior to the mere common employments of domestic life; yet if the flatterer mean to substitute no higher line of occupation in their stead, is it not probable that unhappiness, if not a dereliction from virtue, may be the consequence? Mordaunt's suggestions therefore to a mind more practised in worldly guile would have rendered his intentions extremely equivocal; and the very little Mr. Ross had seen of him made him not only very glad that he was gone, but led him to wish earnestly he might not return; and when a fortnight had elapsed, and no books or packages arrived at the cottage of the Widow Grey, Ross, and, to say the truth, Joanna also, began to hope he would not return. Joanna liked Mordaunt as a companion, and had none of those fears which had crept into the mind of Ross: but her love for her brother, and the certainty that Mordaunt was preferred to him by Ellen, gave her a sort of prejudice against him, and she could not help shewing a sort of triumph at his not returning. Ellen, whose temper was as sweet as her understanding was excellent, bore the little taunts Joanna now and then threw out on her supposed disappointment with great mildness; but when Joanna accused Mordaunt of caprice and insincerity, she sometimes defended him, with candour indeed, but with a little warmth, which excited fresh displeasure in Joanna: and these little disputes insensibly abated the pleasure they used to feel in the society of each other. Nothing could be more ill-judged than Joanna's conduct on this occasion: had she remained silent, Ellen would never have spoken and seldom thought of Mordaunt; but by being forced continually to defend either herself or him, he became more interesting to her; her generous heart not bearing to hear him accused probably without a cause: thus, Joanna, like all people who suffer themselves to be misled by prejudice and ill-humour, increased the evil she wished to obviate, and by rendering her own society less desirable to Ellen, left her more at liberty to receive Mordaunt's visits, if he really should return; and to return it seemed probable at length he intended: for, about three weeks after his departure, several large packages were brought in a light cart to the Widow Grey's, and the driver said he had been hired at Carnarvon, by a strange gentleman who arrived in the mail the night before, and would be with her the next morning. The news of this important event spread quickly through the village, and numerous were the conjectures which followed. Dame Grey had several visitors in the course of the evening to look at these wonderful packages, to conjecture what each might contain, and to endeavour to learn from her what could make a gentleman, so grand as Mr. Mordaunt must be, to come and live in her cottage: to all which the good woman could only reply, that Mr. Ross had told her that the gentleman was coming for his health, and she dared say Mr. Ross knew: at all events, it was nothing to her: the gentleman had agreed to give her twelve shillings a week for her two rooms, which was four shillings more than she expected; but then, to be sure, she was to cook for him, and they all knew she was as pretty a cook as Madam Ross herself; for that, when she lived with 'Squire Davies— The mention of 'Squire Davies was enough for the whole audience; they walked off one by one, and left her to admire and wonder at her lodger's grand packages by herself, dreading nothing more than the tedious tales they knew they must encounter if they staid, now Dame Grey had begun to talk of the days when she lived with 'Squire Davies.

Dame Grey not knowing very well what to do respecting her lodger's rooms, which wanted linen, and many other articles she supposed the packages might contain, thought it would be but right, and the proper compliment, if she was to step up and ask Madam Ross and Miss Joanna, and Miss Ellen, if she were there, what she had better do. Mrs. Ross advised her on no account to open any of the parcels, and said, if Mr. Mordaunt did not arrive in time the next day, she would furnish her with linen proper for his bed and table, till his own could be opened: at the same time declaring her readiness to go with Dame Grey, and see that things were put a little out of a litter; to which obliging act she was certainly prompted by the same sort of curiosity as had influenced her poorer neighbours, to see the packages, and judge by their weight and size what they might contain. No one who has ever lived in a small village will wonder at this: such a one will know that no one creature ever appears in a gown of a different colour, or a hat of a different size from what has been seen before, without exciting the utmost curiosity and animadversion; that a wedding, a burial, or a christening, will afford conversation to the whole neighbourhood for many hours; and that if one should be convicted of living, in the most simple concerns, at all different from the generality, oddity, absurdity, stinginess, and, finally, madness, will probably be imputed to him: think then what a feast for the gossips Mr. Mordaunt's parcels must have presented; for by the time Dame Grey and Mrs. Ross arrived, two or three more were in waiting to take a peep at them. Now, amongst these parcels, &c. was one which certainly bore the appearance of being a lady's bonnet-box: "Well," Mrs. Ross said, "this is an odd thing; what can it contain? Sure Mr. Mordaunt is not going to bring a lady with him! He did not say any thing to you, Dame Grey, did he, as if he was married?" "Lord bless me, no, Madam; but, to be sure, Mr. Ross knows, or Farmer Powis." "Poh! they know nothing at all about it: well, we shall see. For my part I should not wonder: he is not a very young man, and most likely is or has been married." Away went two or three of the assembly, eager to spread the report that Mr. Mordaunt and his lady were coming next day to Dame Grey's; that it must be true, for Madam Ross had said so, and moreover, they had seen with their own eyes *Madam Merdan's* fine bonnet-box, which no doubt contained a power of good things. Some went so far as to settle the probable colour of the lady's bonnet and best gown; and one notable dame, the wife of a farmer, who rented lands adjoining Powis's, thought she would "just step in and tell Miss Ellen and Miss Joanna, that they might smarten themselves a bit, before *Madam Mording* arrived." To paint the surprize of Ellen and Joanna, who were sitting together when neighbour Price related all these strange circumstances, embellished by her own conjectures and comments, would be impossible. Joanna believed, and was not sorry: Ellen doubted, and said she should be glad if it proved so, as Mrs. Mordaunt would be an agreeable addition to their society. Joanna looked at her with arch and half triumphant eyes; and Ellen, teazed, vexed, and disconcerted, could scarcely refrain from tears. At last the chattering gossip departed, and Joanna's conversation with Ellen ran in the usual strain; but Ellen was unusually unable to endure it. Amongst other things, Joanna told Ellen, if Mrs. Mordaunt came, she supposed her whole time would be engaged with her; and if she did not, perhaps she would think Mordaunt's company quite enough without the addition of hers, and that her mother was convinced she would no longer be as willing to be ruled by her as formerly. Ellen now burst into tears, and told Joanna she knew not what she had done to occasion such very unkind remarks; that she had never given her reason to suppose she did not prefer her company to that of any other person, nor ever, for a moment, hesitated to obey Mrs. Ross in all things: but if it was required of her to give up all acquaintance with a man who had never done any thing to offend her, she must say she could not, nay, would not do it. Joanna, startled by a warmth she had not expected from the generally mild and yielding Ellen, now begged her pardon; and embracing her tenderly, said, she knew she had been wrong in teazing her so much, and would in future drop the subject. Ellen's warm forgiving heart immediately prompted her to say she had perhaps herself been captious; and after an appointment to meet again to-morrow, they parted better friends than they had been for a long time.

On Joanna's arrival at home, she inquired of her mother the foundation of the strange story she had heard from Mrs. Price; and could hardly help laughing when she learnt on what slight grounds the report had been raised. Mrs. Ross, however, still defended the probability of her own conjectures, and added, that she was, however, quite sure there were a great many books among the parcels, and she supposed she should now have less work done than ever, for that both Joanna and Ellen would never be easy, unless they were walking with Mordaunt, or reading some of the new trumpery he had sent down. "Dear mother," said Joanna, "why should you think so? You know I am not so very fond of reading, though I like it very well in turn, and should still more, if I had not so many other things to do: and as to Ellen, though I believe she has more pleasure in reading than any thing else in the world; yet you know she is so good and gentle, she never refuses to do any thing you wish her to do." "Aye! that has been; but mark my words, Joanna, you will see alterations you do not expect." This was one of those equivocal prophecies by which Mrs. Ross, like the Vicar of Wakefield, endeavoured to impress her family with an opinion of her penetration: she did not succeed so well as Dr. Primrose, for Mr. Ross never paid the smallest attention to them: and Joanna had so rarely seen one of them fulfilled, that she generally thought nothing about them. In the present instance, however, she certainly felt a little uneasy, and began to fear that poor Charles must forego all hopes of Ellen Powis: for Joanna was in her own mind convinced that Mordaunt greatly admired Ellen, and she was sure Ellen thought him a being of a superior order: and Joanna was too innocent and too unsuspicious to imagine, for a moment, that if Mordaunt liked Ellen, he could have any view but marriage. Ellen, on her side, felt more vexation this night than she could well account for: she could hardly doubt the truth of what Mrs. Price asserted to have heard from Mrs. Ross, namely, that Mordaunt was married, and his lady coming to Llanwyllan with him, this she fancied she should be very glad of: but then she was hurt that Mordaunt should have kept this circumstance a profound secret, and never once adverted to it when he talked, as he had done repeatedly during the two last days of his stay at Llanwyllan, of the pleasure he proposed to himself in the society of Mr. Ross, Ellen, and Joanna.

CHAP. V.

And with them words of so sweet breath composed
As made the things more rich.

HAMLET.

Ellen was engaged the next morning with her needle when Mordaunt suddenly entered the room (for the ceremony of announcing visitors was never thought of at Llanwyllan): she rose hastily, as hastily sat down again, turned pale, then red, and in answer to his hasty inquiries, said—"Are you alone, Sir?" "Alone," replied Mordaunt, surprized beyond measure; "yes, certainly: did you expect to see anyone with me?" "Yes—no, that is, I thought we were told that Mrs. Mordaunt, that your wife was to come with you." "My wife!" exclaimed Mordaunt, turning first as red and then as pale as Ellen had done, almost in the words of Othello, and perhaps not perfectly unlike him in feeling; "What wife? I have no wife." "I beg your pardon, indeed," said Ellen, "for giving you such a strange reception, but we were really told that your lady was certainly coming with you." "What could have given rise," said Mordaunt, regaining his composure, "to such a ridiculous tale? And did _you_, Ellen, could you believe it?" "I own I thought it strange," replied she, "that you had never mentioned it, and I doubted the truth of the story; but Joanna seemed to credit it, and I was told Mrs. Ross had asserted it, but I daresay," added she, smiling, "that it was one of those gossip's tales of which we have so many in this village." Mordaunt said he was wholly unable to account for it, and advancing to the table where she had been sitting, for hitherto they had both continued standing, said—"Shall I disturb you if I sit down by you for half-an-hour?" "Certainly not," said Ellen: "you will allow me to go on with my work." But Ellen's hand did not second her intention, for it shook so much, she was obliged to put down the work, and to say, half laughing, by way of covering her confusion—"I have flurried myself so ridiculously by fancying I was going to see a stranger, that I must rest till my hand is a little more steady." Mordaunt, for the first time, took the trembling hand within his own, and pressing it very gently, said:—"You have not shaken hands with me on my return, Ellen, yet I hoped you would have been glad to see your friend Mordaunt once more: will you allow me the title?" he added, gazing on her intently. Poor Ellen, who had not really any of the usual complimentary phrases, such as "you do me honour, &c." knew neither which way to look nor what to say; and Mordaunt, softly raising her hand to his lips, relinquished it, and pitying her visible confusion, endeavoured to relieve it by saying:—"I think you are a little, a very little paler and thinner than when I left Llanwyllan." "I have been taking a great deal of exercise," said Ellen; "and I think you too, Mr. Mordaunt, are changed: you look pale, and seem fatigued." "Oh yes, Ellen, yes; I have encountered much since we parted—much fatigue both of body and mind. In these sweet shades I hope once more to be at peace: oh, that I might never leave them more, 'the world forgetting, by the world forgot;' that I might, that I could remain here for ever! Would *you*, Ellen, would *you* endeavour to sooth my cares, and to restore my peace of mind?" He again seized her hand, and wildly grasping, pressed it to his throbbing forehead. Ellen looked at him with eyes of apprehension; his energy, his apparent agitation alarmed her: he saw the surprize he had excited, and dropping her hand, said:—"Forgive me, I am not myself to-day; but I must indeed be lost before I can for a moment forget the perfect respect I owe you." His countenance became at once more composed, and after a moment's pause, he said smiling:—"And how is the poor straw hat which I spoilt the night before I went away?" "Indeed you did not spoil it," said Ellen, laughing; "it would not easily be injured." "Oh, certainly, it was completely spoilt, and as I was the author of the mischief, though you would not give me any commission for Bristol or Bath, I could not resist the desire I felt to replace the loss which I know you cannot do here, and I have accordingly chosen one for you, which, though extremely simple, will, I am sure, be particularly becoming: I have also added one for Joanna, not exactly like your's in shape, because it would be ridiculous; I mean it would not be becoming to her style of face." "You are too good: I am sorry you should have had so much trouble." "Oh, the trouble certainly of doing any thing for *you* and your friend must be insupportable; terrible as it was, however, if you will do me the favour of wearing this simple bonnet I shall think it overpaid: there is also a little parcel for Mrs. Ross: and some books for our good friend Mr. Ross: nor have I forgotten my first and truly valued friend your father: his little remembrance I shall take the liberty of sending here; but shall I order the box with the other things to Mr. Ross's or here?" "Mrs. Ross and Joanna are going to pass this afternoon with me," said Ellen; "if you will therefore persist in taking so much trouble, we will examine our presents, which are, I dare say, very elegant." "I thank you a thousand times for not reproving my presumption in fancying I could chuse a hat for you. I will send the box presently, and when the contents have been looked at, may I join your little party and walk with you?" "Certainly; we shall be glad of your company." Mordaunt soon after went away, though Powis, who came in, and seemed heartily glad to see him, pressed him to partake their homely fare at dinner, but promising to come again in the afternoon, Mordaunt declined staying then. Powis was haunted by no fears on his daughter's account: his open hospitable temper made him always ready to receive the stranger, and he saw not far enough into the human heart to suspect that one so eminently gifted by nature and improved by art, as Mordaunt was, must have some paramount inducement to fix himself for two or three months amongst the woods of Llanwyllan. Honest, simple, and credulous, he implicitly believed what Mordaunt had told him respecting his health, and the delight he took in the wild scenery around the village; and pleased with his company, would willingly have had him a constant inmate of his house; yet he doated on, and highly appreciated Ellen; but he fancied that Charles Ross had gained her affections, and looked forward to her marriage with him as a thing determined on. Ellen felt a little awkward on the subject of the bonnet, for she had never mentioned to Mrs. Ross or Joanna that Mordaunt had spent two or three hours at the Farm the night before he left Llanwyllan; as to the straw hat, it was, in reality, not injured, although he chose to fancy it was spoilt by way of excuse for ordering another; she, therefore, did not like to mention the circumstance at all, dreading Mrs. Ross's sharp questions and Joanna's looks; in fact, she did not wish to mention the intended presents, and half resolved to appear surprized when the box arrived: this, however, her natural dislike to deceit deterred her from attempting, though Joanna's late conduct had taught her a reserve she never before had felt towards her. The moment dinner was over Ellen went to her chamber, where she took unusual pains in dressing herself as nicely as her very moderate wardrobe would allow; a neat plain white gown or two being the extent of her finery. Mrs. Ross would seldom allow Ellen or Joanna to wear any thing better than a grey stuff, or small printed calico, yet in spite of her expected rebuke, the very best white gown was this afternoon put on; her hair was nicely and delicately arranged under a cap smaller than those she usually wore; for going without a cap or hat, was, in Mrs. Ross's idea, quite bold and improper. Neither Joanna nor Ellen had ever seen a feather or artificial flower, except once, when mere children, Powis had taken them for a few days to Carnarvon, where a few were exhibited; but as to wearing any, they would as soon have thought of putting on diamonds, so different were their simple ideas from those of the very fine ladies we now see every day walking or riding to market, with their ear-rings and necklaces, fine lace frills, green veils, au parasols: expect them soon with foot-boys at their heels. Yet Powis could have given his daughter a thousand pounds; and Ross, though not rich, was in a station of life which might have entitled Joanna to expect some little indulgences, of which, however, she never even thought. Two or three small bows of pale pink ribbon were the only ornament of Ellen's caps, and her slender waist was surrounded by a short sash of the same colour; a bouquet of late roses and jessamine was placed in her bosom; and the gentle agitation of her spirits animated her eyes and complexion: she looked exquisitely lovely; so fresh—so new—so bright—the poet might have said of her—"she looked like Nature in the world's first spring." She had just completed her nosegay, when Mrs. Ross and Joanna arrived; the former with a new assortment of work prepared for Ellen's completion, who sighed when she saw the quantity to be executed. "Bless me, Ellen," said Mrs. Ross; "why you are dressed up as fine as a lady; one would think you were going to a wedding or a christening.—I hope you have not invited Mrs. Price and Mrs. Howel to-day," (the wives of two neighbouring farmers, who drank tea once or twice a year with Ellen and the Ross's) "for I am come in my old gown, and Joanna in her every-day cotton: why, child, are you dressed so much?" "I don't know, ma'am: I thought my coloured gown was dirty, and the day was so fine and warm, I thought this would be cooler." "Umph," said Mrs. Ross, looking at her with eyes sharpened by curiosity, and then nodding at Joanna, as much as to say you see I was right, she drew up her head and was silent a moment; then, by her next question, shewing the turn her thoughts had taken, she said: "Has Mr. Mordaunt been here?" "Yes, ma'am," said poor Ellen, blushing like crimson. "Umph," again said Mrs. Ross, and again she nodded at Joanna. Joanna, looking slily at Ellen, added, while she could hardly refrain from laughing—"And his wife?" "No," said Ellen, looking up at Joanna, and smiling, for she could not help being diverted at the oddity of her tone and look. Just at this moment in came the maid with a small parcel and a large bonnet-box, which, she said, a boy had brought from Dame Grey's. "God bless my heart," said Mrs. Ross, "why that is the very box I saw at Mr. Mordaunt's, and which made me fancy he was married." Ellen explained as well as she could, but certainly not very clearly, what the contents were; and Joanna was so diverted with the absurdity of the report raised by such a trifle, that she burst into a loud and incontrollable fit of laughing, in which Ellen heartily joined; and though Mrs. Ross scolded, and was quite angry that they would not cease laughing and open the box, they laughed on, when the door opened, and in came Mordaunt. He supposed the box had been received and opened an hour before, not knowing his messenger had stopped to play by the way, and was quite astonished to see them gathered round it, the two girls laughing, and Mrs. Ross half scolding and half laughing too. He was hastily retreating; but his presence operated like an electric shock on the whole party. Ellen was half ashamed; and Mrs. Ross and Joanna, who always felt a degree of awe from the dignity of his manner, were afraid he would be offended: the former endeavoured to explain the cause of their mirth; and Mordaunt no sooner heard what had given rise to the report which had so much perplexed him, than—"Albeit unused to the laughing mood," he could not keep his countenance. The explanation, however, was not unpleasant to him, for he had been quite at a loss to guess how any report of him, whether true or false, could have reached Llanwyllan. The box was now opened, a ceremony at which Mordaunt would willingly not have been present, though he certainly wished to see whether the hat was becoming to Ellen.

Both hats were of straw, equally fine; but that intended for Ellen had an elegant simplicity in the form, which seemed made on purpose for her. At the bottom of the box was found a parcel, directed for Mrs. Ross, which contained a handsome dark sarsnet for a gown, with which the good lady was so delighted, that she quite overwhelmed Mordaunt with thanks and compliments, to which he put a stop by requesting to see the bonnets on their respective owners.

"I am not dressed fit to wear such a bonnet," said Joanna, glancing her eyes on Ellen; "but—" "Aye," said Mrs. Ross, "very true: I believe you knew your bonnet was trimmed with pale pink, Ellen, and put on those ribbons on purpose to match it." "No, indeed," said Ellen, half hurt at the suggestion. Mordaunt saw with what unusual care she was adorned, and could not help being pleased at it. He was himself drest with particular nicety, and was really as handsome and fine a figure as Ellen was beautiful. The bonnets were tried on, and highly approved. Ellen, indeed, was, if possible, improved by hers. The parcel for Powis contained some handsome articles of plate likely to be useful to him; and Mr. Ross's books, which were sent to the Parsonage, consisted of Eschylus, Euripides, and Sophocles, uniformly and elegantly bound, and of superior editions. Thus the taste of all parties seemed to have been consulted, and every one of course was pleased with the kind attention.

CHAP. VI.

To me be Nature's volume broad display'd;
And to peruse its all instructing page,
Or haply catching inspiration thence,
Some easy passage raptured to translate,
My sole delight.

She lov'd: but such her guileless passion was,
As in the dawn of time, inform'd the heart
Of innocence and undissembling truth.

THOMSON'S SEASONS.

From this time Mordaunt's visits at Llanwyllan Farm were constant, and in spite of Mrs. Ross's expected reprehension, Ellen, though always gentle, humble, and submissive, certainly did not execute all the needlework planned for her to do; and, worse than that, Farmer Howel's wife declared she had not above half the usual number of chickens to carry to market for Ellen Powis that she used to have; and Mrs. Ross requesting to taste the currant wine, made under her own direction, found that it had latterly been managed so ill, that it would all become vinegar. This was a grievous fault, and grievously did Ellen answer it, for loud and sharp were Mrs. Ross's animadversions; and repeatedly did she remind Joanna that she had prophesied all this. Joanna walked sometimes with Ellen, and of course with Mordaunt, for they seemed inseparable, but found their conversation frequently turning on things beyond her comprehension, or interrupted by short dialogues, carried on in a low voice, to which her presence seemed an interruption; yet no one could say Mordaunt ever directed himself but with the most entire respect towards Ellen, and politeness towards Joanna. Amongst other wonders which Mordaunt shewed to Ellen, such as beautiful drawings, trinkets for gentlemen, &c. and which were to her entirely new, was one which excited in her, not only admiration, but delight. This was his own miniature picture, beautifully painted, and a striking likeness. Ellen had literally never seen a portrait, except some old faded family pictures, which hung in the hall and staircase of her father's house, and represented some of the former proprietors: but these dull miserable daubs hardly conveyed to her an idea of the delightful art of portrait painting; and when she saw this speaking and elegant resemblance of her fascinating friend, she was so enchanted and enraptured, that Mordaunt, contrary to his first intention, requested her to keep it; and she, ignorant of its value, or the construction the world would have put on her accepting the picture of a gentleman, as readily received it as she had done two or three books and drawings he had given her; but different were the sensations with which she looked at this, to her, most desirable gift: it was the companion of her solitary hours, and, when not actually before her eyes, was ever present to her imagination: and when Mordaunt was absent, his picture was laid by her side; yet a sort of intuitive feeling made her snatch it up, and conceal it when any one approached. It is obvious how greatly this indulgence must have increased those sentiments of tenderness which now so irresistibly assailed her young and innocent heart. As the autumn advanced, and the evenings grew longer, Joanna and Ellen were still left less together. Mordaunt was understood to be continually at the Farm; and even the unobserving farmers' wives began to conclude his attentions into love, and to conclude the match between him and Ellen Powis determined on. A slight cold gave Ellen a reason, or rather an excuse, for staying at home, when at the end of a week Mrs. Ross determined to go herself to the Farm and see how Ellen's work went on. In the road she met Powis, and asking if his daughter were at home, he said, "Yes," and added, "I don't think she is well; she has a cold, and looks pale. How is it you and Joanna have not been to see her these two days?" "Nay," said Mrs. Ross, "I have not seen her for nearly a week. Joanna called the other day, but I fancy Ellen is better engaged than to want *our* company." "How do you mean," said Powis, looking surprized, "why is not Mr. Mordaunt with her every day?" "Why yes, I believe so—part of every day—but what need that hinder your coming? He says she is a clever girl, and she is so anxious to learn what he calls geography, or something like it, that they spend a good deal of their time at their books and such like, and I can't but say I relish my newspaper twice as well now Mr. Mordaunt and Ellen sometimes shew me whereabouts the armies are, and have made me understand whereabouts France, and Spain, and England, and so on are, upon the great maps he has brought to our house."

"'Tis all very well, neighbour Powis, all very well, if you like it: I hope you will have no reason to repent it; but I am afraid, when your shirts and stockings want mending, you will not like these new-fangled ways quite so well." "Why, to be sure, if Ellen neglects her business, that won't do at all; but I assure you she is very industrious, and tells me she rises an hour the earlier every morning, to get through her work, and have time to attend to her books." "Well, neighbour, as long as you are satisfied, I do not wish to make mischief; but certainly Mr. Ross never approved of her or Joanna's learning such things; if he had, he could have instructed them, at least as well as Mr. Mordaunt." "Very true; I did not think of that—well, we will talk to Ellen about it: you will find her at home; I left her busy at work: do speak your mind to her a little; I shall be guided by you and Mr. Ross in all things, seeing you understand such matters better than I do." They then parted, and Mrs. Ross a few minutes after arrived at the Farm; and on walking into the usual sitting-room, instead of finding Ellen at work, she found her surrounded with books and maps, and Mordaunt seated by her side, one arm rested on the back of her chair, while the other was engaged in tracing with the end of his pencil some lines on the map on which Ellen was looking: she was too intently engaged to observe Mrs. Ross's entrance, who stood suspended a moment, while she heard Mordaunt say, "And here, Ellen, here is Northampton—this is the road to Aubyn Castle; and just here——" "What here?" said Ellen, eagerly placing her finger on the spot she supposed to be that on which Mordaunt's habitation stood. "Is it here your house stands?" "Very near that precise spot," replied Mordaunt, drawing her hand gently away, and retaining it in his own, while his expressive eyes were fixed on her face: "very near it is my residence; but it is so far from Llanwyllan, that I begin to detest it, and to dread the thoughts of returning to it.—But what am I doing?" said he, with a deep sigh: "Oh, Ellen, I dare not tell you all my thoughts!" Ellen blushed, sighed, withdrew her hand, and accidentally glancing her eyes upwards, saw Mrs. Ross standing in the door-way, with astonishment, anger, and vexation, painted on her countenance. Ellen started, half screamed, and rose so hastily, she almost overset the table before her. "Bless me, Ma'am," she exclaimed, "I did not see you—I did not know— " "No, I dare say not, Miss Ellen; you were a great deal too much engaged to see or think of me: your servant, Sir. I beg I may not keep you standing; at least *I* shall sit down, for *I* am not going yet."

This gentle hint was intended to tell Mordaunt that she meant to outstay him; but she looked at Ellen with "eyes so full of anger," and Ellen turned so pale, and looked so alarmed, that Mordaunt thought he would at least give Mrs. Ross time to cool a little, before he left them together. Ellen began, in much confusion, to gather the books and maps together. "I am sorry to disturb you, but I did not expect," said Mrs. Ross, "to find you engaged in this manner, at this time of day, whatever you might chuse to do in an evening. I met your father, and he told me you were busy at work, or in the dairy: but," added she, in a low voice, "those things are not thought of *now*." "Indeed, Ma'am," said Ellen, blushing, while the tears started in her eyes, at being so lectured before Mordaunt, "indeed, I had just finished what I had to do in the dairy to-day, and had begun the work you desired me to do, when Mr. Mordaunt accidentally came in, and the maps we had been looking at last night lying in the window, he was just shewing me—" "Oh, it is all mighty well," interrupted Mrs. Ross; "I have no authority to interfere, I am sure, and do not wish to be impertinent. Pray, Sir," added she, turning to Mordaunt, "*do you stay much longer at Llanwyllan?*" "So," thought Mordaunt, "my turn is coming next. I hope, Madam," added he, smiling, "I shall not stay long enough to tire my friends." "Oh, I dare say not, Sir; I dare say you are *pretty sure of that.*" This coarse and cruel hint covered Ellen with the deepest crimson; and Mordaunt, while his face was scarlet, and his eyes sparkled with an indignation he with difficulty repressed, said, in a lofty tone, "I have not, at least, Madam, been accustomed to incur such a misfortune, and therefore flatter myself I have now done nothing to deserve it." He rose with dignity, and approaching Ellen, who sat almost motionless, he took her trembling hand, bowed respectfully upon it, and said, "I shall do myself the honour of attending your father and yourself, Miss Powis, in the evening." Then slightly bowing to Mrs. Ross, he departed. "Good lack, good lack," said Mrs. Ross, who, awed by his manner, had been silent a moment, "what a dainty speech! The honour of attending Miss Powis! well, what will this world come to! Why, Ellen, child, you are spoilt for a farmer's wife, and will soon begin to fancy yourself a lady indeed." Ellen, whose spirits were now totally subdued, wept bitterly, and said, "I am sure, Madam, I do not know how I have deserved to be treated thus."

Softened by her distress, for with all her sharpness, Mrs. Ross loved Ellen, and really had her welfare at heart, she began to relent, and said more softly, "Why now, Ellen, child, hear me. Do you think it is right or creditable for a young girl like you to be constantly receiving the visits of such a man as Mr. Mordaunt? Tell me, Ellen, will he make you his wife?"

This was a question Ellen had never dared to ask herself. In the beautiful language of Shakespeare, which Mordaunt had lately given her, and with which she was so enchanted, she often allowed herself only three hours sleep in a night, that she might find time to read, she had often repeated to herself—

—— It were all one,
That I should love a bright particular star,
And think to wed it: he is so above me;
In his bright radiance, and collateral light
Must I be comforted, not in his sphere.

This question from Mrs. Ross, therefore, struck her heart with a pang of unutterable anguish, and she felt almost dying, while she owned, that so far from offering her his hand, Mordaunt had never spoken one word of love to her. Mrs. Ross, however, was rather pleased at the latter part of this confession, for she began to fear worse for the innocent and guileless Ellen than the capture of her heart; that, she had no doubt, might soon be retrieved when Mordaunt quitted the country, and Ellen could have no farther acquaintance with him; but she had begun to fear that his views were such as might involve Ellen in infamy, as well as misfortune: these fears, however, she had feeling enough to conceal from their object, and only dwelt upon the trouble she was preparing for herself, by giving so much of her time and regard to a man who, it evidently appeared, had no thoughts of her. In vain did Ellen murmur the word "Friendship," and faintly protest neither Mordaunt nor herself had the least idea of any thing beyond. Mrs. Ross, though her knowledge of the world was not extensive, knew enough to be convinced of the fallacy of such pretensions, and she ceased not till she drew from the dejected Ellen a promise to see less of Mordaunt, and to regain, as speedily as possible, her former mode of life. "And let me, Ellen, also, see you looking blooming and merry again," said she. "I wish, with all my heart, this man had never found his way to Llanwyllan: you used to be active, industrious, and happy; not a care to distress you, not a trouble to take away your colour; but now Charles would not know you again." "Charles!" thought Ellen, while a strange feeling, not unmingled with indignant comparison, swelled her heart, and gave a transient colour to her cheek. "What is Charles to me? Why am I always to be teased about him? They will teach me to hate, instead of loving him." "Well, Ellen, may I suppose you will take my advice?" "Certainly, Ma'am," said Ellen, with a deep sigh; "but," added she, hesitating, "you know, Ma'am, Mr. Mordaunt said he would be here this evening. You would not wish me—it would look very particular, very rude." "Never mind that. Come, you say you have done all you had to do in the dairy, so put on your hat, take your work, and come and dine with us like a good girl, as you used to be; you can leave word you were obliged to go out, and the sooner you let him see you are determined to avoid him the better." Ellen dared not refuse; she hesitated some excuse about her father's dining alone, which Mrs. Ross obviated by saying he would only run home, and take his dinner, and out again, and would not want her. Waiting, therefore, while poor Ellen put on her hat, and bathed her eyes, she dragged her away with her, and kept her all day at the Parsonage. Nay, under pretence of finishing their work, she would not suffer either Ellen or Joanna to stir out, though the weather was beautiful. Late in the evening Mr. Ross came in; he spoke with such particular kindness, and in so soothing a tone to Ellen, that the tears, which she had with difficulty restrained all day, ran down her cheeks, and she hastily rose, under pretence of looking at the moon, and went to the open window: there leaning her head over the window-seat, into which the jasmine crept, she hoped the torrents of tears she was shedding might fall unobserved; but the good Ross, who had followed her, and now stood at a small distance from her, perceived, by her air and action, that she was weeping, though no one else noticed it; for Ellen's was

"Mute, silent sorrow, free from female noise,
Such as the majesty of grief destroys."

He was distressed to see her sorrow, and gently approaching, he took her hand, (while she, half starting, turned her head aside) and said, "My dear Ellen, I lament to see you so dejected; assure yourself, we love you as our own child, and would in all things consult your happiness. But reflect, my dear, on the change a few short weeks have produced: this man, this Mordaunt; nay, blush not, Ellen; for who can doubt it is on his account you weep—I own him elegant in person, polished in manners,

"Complete in person and in mind,
With all good grace to grace a gentleman!"

"But what has he been to you? A friend! No, Ellen; he found you cheerful, contented with your lot, and happily engaged in the active duties of your station. What has he done for you? He has inspired you with views above the state where Providence has placed you. He has made your former useful occupations, your former simple friends, insipid to you; he has sought to give a degree of refinement to your taste, of delicacy to your sentiments, of which I well know nature has made you fully capable; but unless he means to transplant you to a soil where these flowers may flourish, believe me, Ellen, he has done you no kindness. He has only prepared for you years of anguish, of vain regret, of useless discontent, which will for ever destroy not only the glow upon your cheek, but the spring and elasticity of your mind. I will not ask you what are his professions; I will only suppose, that if they are serious, your father and your friends would not be strangers to them."

Here Ellen sunk into a chair, and sobbed aloud. Mrs. Ross and Joanna, seeing that Ross was talking to her, had stolen out of the room. "It grieves me to distress you, my dear girl," said the benevolent Ross, and his gentle voice became tremulous; "but, Ellen, let my experience benefit you. There are characters in the world of which your innocent nature can form no idea. I will not offend your delicacy, nor indeed my own belief, by supposing, for an instant, that Mordaunt is one of those villains who seek the seduction of innocence."

Here Ellen started from her chair, her clasped hands, glowing cheeks, and throbbing bosom, bespeaking an indignant agitation, which would not be controlled. Ross, gently reseating her, said, "Ellen, I wrong not you; I wrong not him, so much as to imagine such a possibility; but there are men, who, though they lead not so decidedly to guilt, yet lead as certainly to misery acute as aught but guilt can make it: and that only for the gratification of a mean and sordid vanity, inconceivable by such as have not witnessed its effects. I had once a sister, Ellen, fair almost as yourself, as gentle, and as virtuous; possessed of a sensibility that was at once her grace and her misfortune. In early life, it fortuned that she met with one of those practised deceivers, who united talents the most superior to manners the most enchanting. By a long series of quiet and silent attentions, by studying her tastes, devoting his time to her, he, without ever addressing to her a word of love, led her, and all who knew her, to believe he was her lover, and would be her husband. At last she was told that such was his usual practice, when he met with any woman who was superior to those around her; but she felt indignant at the accusation, and would not believe it till that belief was forced upon her, by seeing him going over the same ground with another. 'She pined in thought;' and a hectic complaint, to which she was subject, gained fast upon her. A mutual friend came to an explanation with him, while the mean wretch declared he had never made any profession to her, and never even thought of marrying her; but that the world would talk, and he wondered she did not despise it, as he did. A few months terminated the existence of the injured creature. Sweet Emily! thy gentle spirit fled to those regions where no deceit could further betray thee. The wretch at last met his fate in a duel with the brother of one whom he had sought to mislead, as he had done the unfortunate Emily." Ross's voice here failed, and both were silent. "Assure yourself, Ellen," at length resumed Ross, "I was not blind to your talents, and your love of knowledge; and many have been my struggles against the strong inclination I felt to become your instructor. My own children had not, I easily saw, such minds as yours, and I longed to cultivate your vigorous understanding. I resisted, though the temptation was aided by the wish I felt to secure to myself a future companion and assistant in the studies I best loved. Why, Ellen, did I resist? What was the powerful motive which prevented my yielding to such united inducements? It was a wish to secure your welfare and your happiness, which I thought would be most certainly effected by limiting your acquirements to something like an equality with those amongst whom you seemed fated to live. I may have erred in judgment; and since the bent of your inclination so determinately points towards the acquisition of knowledge, I am willing to suppose that I have done so. I will then, Ellen, be your tutor: we will, with Mrs. Ross's assistance, so arrange your hours, that your new employments shall not interfere with your domestic duties; and let me hope, my dear, that the same strength of mind, which so eagerly leads you to literary pursuits, will be manifested in conquering any sentiment too tender for your peace, which may have been excited by one, who, I fear, has merely had in view his own gratification. Should I wrong him—should he hereafter prove that he feels a sincere affection for you, and seeks your happiness, great will be my joy: no selfish or personal consideration shall influence my wishes on this subject. I had hoped that Charles might have been happy with the object of his first affections; but that I see is not *at present* likely: fear, therefore, no persecution on that subject, either from me, or his mother and sister."

Ross was silent; and Ellen, who had hitherto remained so from the mingled feelings of pride, regret, and tenderness, which swelled her heart, now fearing to seem sullen, faintly articulated, "You are very good and kind: I will be all I can—all, if possible, you wish me to be."

Ross, seeing the variety of emotions she had that day undergone had quite exhausted her, advised her to retire to bed, saying she had better sleep there, and in the morning they would talk a little further on her future plans. Ellen, however unwillingly, how much soever her rebellious heart longed to return home, in the hope of seeing Mordaunt if but for a minute, yet felt that Ross had acted so kindly and so wisely, that his reasoning was so founded on truth, that she determined "in all her best to obey him." She retired therefore to the chamber she and Joanna had so often occupied, when no care disturbed their repose, when "sleep sat upon her eyes, peace in her breast." But ah! how changed! Exhausted, wan, and spiritless; her eyes heavy with weeping; her heart agitated with a thousand contending reflections, Ellen long vainly sought repose. Joanna was unusually kind and affectionate—she said little; and all she said was tender and endearing. Ellen felt truly grateful for this goodness, and found her love for her early friend revive, now the roughness which abated it was once more laid aside. At length, thoroughly wearied with the occurrences of the day, "tired Nature's kind restorer—balmy sleep," came to her aid, "and steeped her senses in forgetfulness."

CHAP. VII.

Grief was heavy at her heart,
And tears began to flow!
Soft as the dew from heaven descends,
His gentle accents fell.

GOLDSMITH'S HERMIT.

In the morning Mrs. Ross and Joanna left Mr. Ross and Ellen together for a few minutes: he drew his chair close to hers, and said, "Do not think, Ellen, I wish to tease or distress you; but tell me, will it not be better that you remain our guest for the present? You cannot, when left alone at Llanwyllan, refuse to admit Mr. Mordaunt without a particularity which it is on all accounts better to avoid: but here, even if he comes, you may see him with propriety; and when he finds no opportunity of entertaining you alone, he will probably cease to visit us, and perhaps leave Llanwyllan altogether." His mild expressive eyes glanced over Ellen's countenance: he saw her shrink and tremble at the painful idea he had excited; and while her every feature expressed the most exquisite anguish, the good man gently sighed, and removing his eyes from her face, endeavoured to conceal his knowledge of her distress. As he seemed to wait her answer, Ellen made a strong effort, and said, "The plan you propose, Sir, is undoubtedly the best: if you will be troubled with me, I will remain as long as you please." This matter settled, Ross undertook to reconcile Powis to spare Ellen for a short time; and reading her apprehensions in her countenance, said softly, "Fear not: I will give him sufficient reasons, without exciting his displeasure, or even his suspicion of our real motive." Ross accordingly went to the Farm, and meeting with Powis in one of the fields near the house, he told him that Ellen was not quite well, though better than she had been the night before, and therefore his wife wished to detain her a few days at the Parsonage to remove her cold, and would herself visit the Farm for an hour or two, to settle the concerns of the dairy, poultry-yard, &c. &c. and that they should be very glad to see him in the evening, or at any of their meals, when he could make it convenient. These little arrangements between the two families had till very lately been so frequent, that Powis felt not the least surprize, though he owned he was sorry Ellen had not come home the night before, as Mr. Mordaunt had seemed rather hurt about it; "And he has been so very civil and kind, you know, neighbour Ross, that one would not wish to affront him." So perfectly unsuspicious was this good man, that not a thought crossed his mind of the possible intention of Mordaunt's visits; and secure in Ellen's fancied affection for Charles Ross, he never dreamt of her thinking of any other man. Ross silently acquiesced in what he said, and then went into the house to deliver some directions to the servant, and which, he said, Mrs. Ross should go herself in the course of the day to see executed. In the common sitting-room Ross found the maps and books at which Mordaunt and Ellen had been looking the preceding day (his wife had told him the circumstances of her visit): he was rather surprized at the neatness and even elegance of their binding, though merely what might be called school-books in geography and grammar, and found that the maps were excellent and expensive. On the window lay a beautifully bound volume or two of Shakespeare, Thomson's Seasons, marked and underlined at the description of Lavinia, Cowper's Poems, and two or three others; in all of which was written, "Ellen Powis, the gift of her friend Constantine." And in two or three were short passages in Italian and French, written in a small hand with a pencil, expressive of admiration and regard, and evidently applied to Ellen. From one of them dropt the following

STANZAS TO THE MOON.

Oh, thou bright moon! whose beams, however fair,
So lately my sad eyes unheeding saw;
Whose soothing light from its unceasing care,
My heavy soul so vainly strove to draw;
I bid thee witness now, that pale despair,
Her comfortless dominion o'er my mind,
Reluctant yields, and hope begins to share,
The empire of my soul, with visions kind!

With soften'd feelings on thy beams I gaze,
And their mild influence stealing on my heart,
Enchanting visions in my bosom raise,
Sweet friendship comes her blessings to impart:
In Ellen's form she comes! Oh, fairest form!
Oh, sweetest voice, that from the grief-worn soul
E'er stole its cares, e'er bade the beating storm
Of sorrow cease, and could each woe controul!

Several erasures and interlineations proved this to be an original, and probably an unfinished performance.

Ross saw in all this new reason to be alarmed: he no longer wondered at the progress this insinuating man had made in the affections of Ellen, and most earnestly did he wish that Mordaunt had never seen her, or had selected her for his wife. Yet even in that case there was something to consider: they knew nothing of Mordaunt but what he had told them. There was certainly something equivocal in the total retirement of such a man from the world: he might have been driven from it rather by his vices than by his misfortunes: yet there was in the appearance and manners of Mordaunt, an uprightness, a loftiness of carriage, that looked not like that of a man debased and bowed down by guilt. While Ross thus meditated, Mordaunt suddenly came in—his eyes sparkling, and his cheeks glowing: for hearing some one moving in the parlour, and having seen Powis in the fields at a distance, he concluded it could be no one but Ellen: his impatient step, extended hand, and pleased countenance, at once explained to Ross what his expectation had been. On seeing him, Mordaunt half started back, exclaiming, "I thought——" Then recovering himself, he again advanced, and offering his hand to Mr. Ross, said with much cordiality, "My dear Sir, I am glad to see you: it is sometime since we met." There was a charm in the voice and manner of Mordaunt that few could withstand, however unkindly disposed towards him. Ross, who had from the first felt pleased with him, although he now on Ellen's account was angry, yet could not prevail on himself to appear displeased; yet there was a coolness in his expression that was visible enough to so acute an observer as Mordaunt. Whatever was his motive, however, he chose not to notice it, but continued to speak with frankness and vivacity, inquiring for Mrs. Ross and Joanna. At last, glancing his eyes round the room, he said, "Are you alone this morning, my good Sir? Miss Powis, I learnt, slept at your house last night: I hope she is not ill?" Through all the assumed composure of his look, and affected indifference of his tone, Ross plainly saw that Mordaunt made this inquiry with real anxiety; but of the true motive of that anxiety he was extremely doubtful. He replied somewhat coldly, "Ellen is certainly not quite well, and Mrs. Ross thinks her *safest* under her own *care at present.*" This speech, which might to a guilty conscience have conveyed "more than met the ear," seemed to be literally interpreted by Mordaunt; and thrown off his guard, he evinced great agitation, while he exclaimed, "Safest! Good God! You do not surely apprehend any danger in her complaints?" "Not exactly that," said Ross (not displeased at his warmth), "but she has a bad cold; and Mrs. Ross has a high opinion of her own skill as a nurse: we shall therefore keep Ellen with us for a few days at least. If she should then not be better, I shall advise her father to let her change the air."

This suggestion seemed to complete the dismay of Mordaunt: he trembled, and turned pale. Ross, bowing, wished him "good morning," and walked away. Mordaunt, after a moment's recollection, followed him hastily, and as they walked, endeavoured to enter into a more general conversation, apparently in the hope that he was going home, and that by going with him, he might see Ellen: but Ross was going to visit a sick parishioner at some distance. Mordaunt was therefore obliged to take leave of him at the door of his own lodgings: he ventured to say, as they parted, "I shall take an early opportunity of inquiring for my friends at the Parsonage, Mr. Ross." In answer to which Ross bowed, and said, but not very cordially, he should be glad to see him.

"And must I bear all this!" said Mordaunt, as they parted: "to what have I reduced myself? Yet this, and more, sweet Ellen, will I bear for thee! Yet to what purpose? Can I, dare I, link thee to such a fate as mine may be? Yet can I leave thee, or bear to be so near, and not to see thee? To be forbidden, at least by looks forbidden to approach thee: to encounter the angry glances of a narrow-minded woman, and even by her benevolent husband to be received with coldness almost bordering on contempt? Yes, Ellen, I will bear it all! Would to heaven they would have left us to ourselves, till time—till the full conviction of her affection—they need not have feared." Thus in broken sentences murmured Mordaunt, as he strode impatiently across his narrow apartment, and determined nothing should prevent him from seeing Ellen, and ascertaining whether Ross's fears for her health were not merely a pretence for separating them.

The whole day passed heavily with Ellen, yet Mrs. Ross and Joanna were unusually kind to her: no hinted doubt, no implied accusation of herself and Mordaunt met her ear; but her heart was ill at ease, and her forced employments irksome. She longed to lie in her own quiet parlour, where, if Mordaunt might not come, at least she might think of him without restraint. Ross returned to dinner: he took no notice of Ellen's dejection, nor mentioned having met with Mordaunt; but told her he had seen her father, who was quite satisfied she should stay with them awhile, and try to recover her health, and that he thought it probable they should see him in the evening. As the afternoon was remarkably clear, and not too warm (for the autumn was by this time far advanced), he invited the girls to walk with him, instead of resuming their work, to which Mrs. Ross gave her consent without a murmur, only begging they would not walk too far, as she thought Ellen not strong enough to bear much fatigue. To this they agreed, and Ellen found the calm soft air revive her. Ross led the conversation to the wonders of nature: he explained in familiar terms the structure of some flowers he gathered, and made them admire the wisdom of that Being, who had formed those blossoms so exquisitely fair. Thence he descanted on the nature and properties of some rare plants, and was on all so eloquent and so instructive, that Ellen felt her heart expand more lightly, and some degree of pleasure take possession of her mind. "But ah!" thought she, "why is not Mordaunt partaker of this sweet conversation? Why are two men, so well fitted to gratify and delight each other, thus to be estranged? Surely, Mr. Ross does not properly appreciate either the qualities of Mordaunt's mind, or the excellence of his heart and principles. Had he heard from him the sentiments which have charmed me—did he know the delicacy of his taste, and his abhorrence of every thing mean and base, he could not suppose him the wretch he last night described." Yet Ellen was so candid and unprejudiced, she could allow great reason in many of Ross's suggestions; and her high opinion of his judgment, and the general liberality with which it was exercised, filled her heart with uneasy fears.

They had been a few minutes returned to the house, and were just sitting down to their simple supper, when Powis came in; and hastening to meet Ellen, whom he had not seen for nearly two days, he tenderly kissed her. She loved her father most affectionately, and had met him so eagerly, that she did not for the instant perceive Mordaunt, who had followed him into the room, and advanced towards her. She was startled; and fearing what reception her friends would give him, she turned pale, and trembled, which her father perceiving, said, "Why, Ellen, it is only Mr. Mordaunt: you are not frightened at him, are you? Why, you have not seen him these two or three days, he tells me. Come, shake hands with him, and tell him you are glad to see him." Not for worlds could Ellen have articulated one word; but Mordaunt, taking advantage of her father's friendly commands, took the hand she could not— dared not offer; and pressing it vehemently between his own, said in a low voice, "No, Ellen, do not *say* you are *glad* to see me: the formal coldness of such an expression from you would be worse to me than that averted look which leads me to believe, at least to fear, the sight of me is far from pleasing to you."

A vivid blush spread over her countenance, and she suddenly lifted her eyes to him with an expression of reproachful yet gentle timid affection, that at once explained to him all that her heart was filled with. Joy, delight, and an expression of the most tender love and admiration, took possession of Mordaunt's fine features: he seemed transfixed, and stood gazing on her, still holding her hand, as if he had no longer power over his own actions. "Why, how you stand," said honest Powis, laughing, "staring at one another as if you had never met before! Come, neighbour Ross, I am come to eat a bit of your cold meat: I have been in the fields all the evening, and made but a short dinner, Ellen not being at home. Come, let us sit down, and begin supper."

Nothing could equal the awkwardness of Mordaunt's situation: he felt himself an intruder, yet could not tear himself away. Ross, his wife, and Joanna, had indeed all spoken to him with civility; but there was something in their manner which fully convinced him he was no welcome guest; and though Ellen looked somewhat pale, yet he saw in her no sign of such a state of health as should make her residence with Mrs. Ross necessary. Relieved by this conviction (for he had really been alarmed for her), he yet felt mortified in perceiving that she was kept there on purpose to avoid his visits. At length, a little recovering himself, he relinquished her hand, and said, "Pray let me be no interruption: I am going instantly: I merely called to inquire how Miss Powis was this evening, and am happy to find her not so ill as I feared." He now bowed, and was retiring, when Ross, ashamed of appearing so inhospitable, pressed him to sit down with them; and Joanna (pitying Ellen's confusion, who was quite distressed at her father's apparent surprize at the coolness—to him unaccountable—of Mordaunt's reception), said with great good-nature, "Here's a chair, Mr. Mordaunt; and as you never eat any thing but fruit at night, see what fine peaches and grapes we have."

Mordaunt, charmed by the kind invitation, and by seeing the chair mentioned was placed between herself and Ellen, could not resist the temptation: he sat down, and vainly endeavoured to behave as he used to do: but there was a visible restraint over the whole party, except Powis; and though Ross attempted several times to keep up something like conversation, it soon languished, and every one seemed weary and uneasy—the mind of each was pre-occupied; and what either said, appeared to be far from the thing they were thinking of. Once or twice Mordaunt spoke in a low voice to Ellen; but she, awed by the presence of Mr. and Mrs. Ross, answered only in the briefest way possible, and rarely lifted her eyes from the table. He asked her at last if she should be at home to-morrow. She replied in the negative. "Nor the next day?" "I believe not." "Good God! and how long is this to last?" "I do not know: Mrs. Ross thinks I shall be better here for awhile." "And do you never walk?" "Yes: we walked this evening with Mr. Ross."

Mordaunt saw that every thing possible was done to prevent their meeting, and that he must come to some decision speedily. Of Ellen's love, he could no longer doubt: his own for her he had for some time felt to be that overwhelming sentiment, which must finally conquer all opposing circumstances; but there were such in his fate as ought (at least he thought so) to have prevented him from linking hers with it; yet he had insensibly been so led on, he saw there was no retreating, and determined shortly to come to an explanation with Ross and her father, though much he wished a further time had been allowed. These reflexions, which in spite of himself and the habit of self-command he had so hardly acquired, sank him into silence; and at length, Powis, tired of the gloom and heaviness which seemed hung over the whole party, so different from what their little suppers used to be, told them he thought they were all very stupid, and he would go home and go to bed. Then shaking Ross by the hand, he went round the table to Ellen, kissed her, and wished her good night, telling her to get quite well as fast as possible, for he wanted her at home. Mordaunt bade them good night at the same time, and went away with Powis.

CHAP. VIII.

"Are then the sons of interest only wise?
Can pomp alone essential good impart?
Mistaken world; ah! why thus vainly prize
Those gifts which but contract the human heart?

"Why only *folly* that fond passion call,
Which Heaven itself implanted in the mind;
Links each to each, and, harmonizing all,
Swells the rapt heart with sympathy refin'd."

The reflections of a long and sleepless night determined Mordaunt on the line of conduct he ought to pursue; and as soon as he thought the early breakfast at the Parsonage would be ended, he walked thither, and asking for Mr. Ross, was shewn into the little study, which that good man called exclusively his own. Yet here, in the very last place where he would have expected to find her, to his utter astonishment he saw Ellen. Ellen alone—seated at a table covered with books, from one of which she appeared learning something, or rather to have been so employed, for at the moment he entered her thoughts had wandered; and she was sitting, one fair hand holding the open book, the other covering her eyes. Supposing the person who entered to be Mr. Ross, who had that day commenced the office of her tutor, she looked up; but seeing Mordaunt, the book fell from her hand, and she vainly endeavoured to rise from her seat—a ceremony not yet exploded by the unfashionable inhabitants of Llanwyllan. Mordaunt sprang eagerly forward, exclaiming, "Here Ellen! Good Heavens! could I have hoped to see you here! At last then we meet again, without the irksome restraint of surrounding witnesses, of almost hostile eyes! Fear not, dearest, for ever dearest Ellen." Seeing she looked half alarmed at his unusual warmth, for in general his manner towards her was, though tender, composed,—"fear not: never may word nor look of mine give you reasonable cause of alarm or vexation. Worlds would I give for one hour's uninterrupted conversation with you—but now another moment may prevent my saying more. Tell me then, sweetest girl, may I, will you permit me to apply to Mr. Ross for his interest with you, and with your father, till I can hope that my assiduities, if not my merit, may have excited in you a tenderer sentiment than mere esteem?"

Bewildered—perplexed—hardly knowing or understanding what she heard, or believing that Mordaunt could be in earnest in what she could not but suppose a declaration of his love, Ellen gasped, trembled, and half fainted in his supporting arms.

At this moment Ross entered, and seeing this extraordinary scene, gazed with surprize, almost with dismay, upon them. "I was told," said he, gravely advancing, "that Mr. Mordaunt wished to speak to *me*. What is the matter Ellen? are you ill?" "Forgive my vehemence, dear Ellen," said Mordaunt. "I have startled your tender spirits by my impatience: permit me to conduct you to your friends; or shall Mr. Ross and I retire together?"

The particular tenderness of this address, and this almost open avowal of the interest he took in her, still more and more surprized Ross. Ellen rose, and with difficulty supporting herself, murmured she would go to Mrs. Ross— "Do so," said Ross; "but let *me* assist you.—Mr. Mordaunt, be seated; I will return to you immediately."—Without speaking more to her, he took her arm in his, and having seated her in the parlour, (where fortunately Joanna was alone), he told her to compose herself, and returned to a visitor whom every hour made him think more perplexing and extraordinary. Mordaunt extended his hand, and grasping Ross's within it, said, with noble frankness, "You have been, my dear Sir,—perhaps still are displeased with me: but the time is come when the mysteries which surround me shall be cleared away. If you will grant me your attention for an hour I will relate to you some circumstances upon which I must at present beg you to be silent; but to the truth of all which I pledge myself by every asseveration which can bind the man of principle and honour."

They were seated, and Mordaunt related to Ross many events, and disclosed many secrets, which we shall for the present take leave to pass over. Having finished the astonishing recital, he said, "And now, my dear Sir, having heard all I know of myself, and all I may hereafter fear, will you candidly tell me whether I may hope not only for your consent, but for your good wishes that I may marry Ellen Powis? May I, do you think, venture to make her mine, when perhaps a few months may involve me in so much vexation if not disgrace? And do you think I may hope such a share of affection from her as will reconcile her to future events, of whatever nature they may be?"—"I see," said Ross, "that my cautious fears for her peace have a little precipitated your measures. It might have been better, perhaps, to let things go on quietly till the return of that young man you have mentioned to me from abroad might have explained his future intentions: perhaps his opinions may have altered during his absence: be that as it may, if you were now to leave Llanwyllan without coming to a farther explanation with Ellen, I fear her peace would be too deeply endangered; for though I would scrupulously guard her delicacy, and leave the declaration of her sentiments to her own lips, yet it would be idle to deny my conviction that she has seen her *friend Mordaunt* with what I believe I must call *preference*. Is not that the proper word, think you, Sir?" He smiled, and added such kind professions of regard for Mordaunt, and expressed so much delight at his truly disinterested love for Ellen, as left our traveller nothing to wish from him.

It was determined that not even Ellen should know at present the circumstances Mordaunt had revealed to Ross. "If she knows them," said Mordaunt, "she will think duty calls upon her to impart at least some of them to her father, and we are sure our worthy friend Powis will make no secret of them; you cannot doubt, Mr. Ross, how greatly it would annoy me to have them known while we remain at Llanwyllan; when we are gone, the leading circumstances will not remain a secret long, for I hope for your kind interest with Ellen and her father, that I may take her with me ere long, before winter has rendered travelling over your 'staircase roads,' as some one expresses it, unpleasant, if not unsafe. I am perhaps presuming too far, but I think, I hope, from Ellen's gentle tremor and not repugnant looks, when just now I was hurried into something very like a declaration of my love, though I came purposely to consult you before I made it, that she will not be inexorable." "I think," replied Ross, "I may venture to assure you she will not even affect a hesitation which her heart disclaims. Ellen has been brought up in the most perfect modesty, but at the same time in the most perfect sincerity, and it is really out of her power to conceal her sentiments; and to me, who have known her from her infancy, they are as obvious as if her heart was open to my view; but I will not say more," said he, with a benevolent smile.—"I ought not to betray my darling little pupil: by the bye," added he, turning to the books, &c. "my office of schoolmaster will, I suppose, soon be taken from me; I might as well not have attempted to take it out of your hands." Mordaunt laughed, and asked Ross if he might not request to see Ellen then. "You may easily imagine my anxiety," added he. "Why," said Ross, "there is something so formidable in sending for the poor little girl, and seating her formally to hear what you undoubtedly are impatient to say, that if you can allow her a little time to compose herself, after the flurry she has had this morning already, I really think it will be better. Will you partake of our humble dinner to-day—can you eat at our unfashionable early hour? for the good people here, amongst other things, are amazed at your usual hours; if you can, pray favour me; and after dinner I will so far relax my late vigilance, as to permit you to speak to Ellen apart for ten minutes: will that be long enough?" "Not quite," said Mordaunt, half laughing; "but how shall we manage with Mrs. Ross, who, I believe, holds me in very serious aversion, and with Joanna, who will, I know, have her mother's commands not to stir from Ellen?" "How well you have read us all," said Ross, laughing in his turn: "but trust to me: I will remove all these formidable obstacles—yet do not fancy my good woman has any dislike to you; whatever displeasure she has shewn originated in her vexation at seeing your influence had deranged the plans she thought best for Ellen to pursue, and endangered, as we feared, her happiness; for though she may not shew it exactly according to the manner a more enlightened mind might chuse, assure yourself Mrs. Ross loves Ellen with the affection of a mother." "I doubt it not," replied Mordaunt with vivacity: "who can see and not love that exquisite creature?—what a person—what a mind she has! You may believe, after all I have told you, that 'for several virtues have I liked several women.' I may go on and add, that 'she, so perfectly and so peerless, was created of every creature's best.'"

"Indeed," said Ross, "I have ever highly appreciated Ellen, but I believe not highly enough, for I never thought of her making a conquest so important: the little gipsy is not aware of the power of her charms." "Ah," said Mordaunt, shrinking, "do not lead my thoughts that way, do not let me suppose, if she knew them better, my success with her might be less to be hoped; that when the world shall have taught her to estimate them more highly—" "Ah, beware of jealousy," said Ross. "Name not the horrid word," cried Mordaunt, with some emotion; "too much reason have I to know its misery; but with your virtuous, with your pious Ellen, I shall surely be secure." "Doubt it not," replied Ross, gravely; "if ever human being might be relied on for truth, for sincerity, for singleness of heart, that being is Ellen Powis; yet the world is a dangerous school, and you, I hope, will watch with unceasing care over your inexperienced pupil, whose very virtues may betray her, if not into error, into the appearance of it."

A few more words passed between them, and then Mordaunt retired to dress for dinner, a custom from which he never departed even in this retired spot.

During this long conference, poor Mrs. Ross had been in a complete fidget (to use her own word) to know its subject: her curiosity had long since reached its highest point, and she repeated almost incessantly to Ellen and Joanna, who sat at work beside her,—"Well, what in the whole world can Mr. Mordaunt have to say to Mr. Ross—well, what can they be talking of all this time? Dear, I hope they won't quarrel." "Quarrel!" repeated Joanna, while Ellen's work dropt from her fingers, and she looked amazed and terrified: "quarrel! my dear mother, what should they quarrel about? Besides, did you ever know my father quarrel with anybody?" "No: true enough, he has a very fine temper; but then, *that* Mr. Mordaunt seems so hasty, and sometimes looks so strangely, that—besides, I thought he seemed quite angry when we went away last night." She then opened the parlour door, which was exactly opposite to that of the study, and stood a minute as if to catch the sound of their voices.

"Well, I declare they are talking still, but not loud: bless me! I actually heard one of them laugh." "So much the better, mamma," said Joanna; "I always like to hear people laugh; it shews there is no mischief going on." "Not at all, not at all, Joanna," said Mrs. Ross, whose irritated curiosity disposed her to contradiction. "I am sure I have often thought, when I have heard you two girls chattering and laughing, that you were planning some mischief." "Well, mamma, I am sure we never executed it, for you know we were always the best girls in the world." "Pretty well, pretty well sometimes," replied Mrs. Ross, half smiling in the midst of her bustle.

At length the study door opened, and Mordaunt was seen to pass through the little garden before the house, to which Ross attended him: they shook hands at parting. "You see, mamma, they have not quarrelled," said Joanna; "so far from it, I have a great notion they are better pleased with each other than they have been lately;" and she glanced slily at Ellen, for Joanna had little doubt what subject had employed, at least, part of the time they had been together.

As soon as Mordaunt was gone, Ross came into the parlour, and said,— "What have we for dinner to-day, my dear?" "Well, Mr. Ross, I don't think I ever heard you ask before in all my life." "Possibly not, my dear; but I wish to know, because Mr. Mordaunt dines with us." "Mr. Mordaunt!" repeated Mrs. Ross: "well, of all things, that is the last I should have expected. Why, *now* I am surprized indeed:—then we have such an odd dinner to-day;— nothing but——" "Never mind, my dear, never mind, you can easily make a little alteration: come with me, and I will tell you more; in the meantime, girls, go and make yourselves very smart. Mr. Mordaunt is only gone home to dress, and will be here again soon; of course, as he is so nice in his own appearance, he will expect to find you lasses dressed to receive him." "Dear Mr. Ross," said the good woman, staring at him, "I do not know you to-day! What in the world is come to you? First you inquire about dinner, and then you tell the girls to go and dress themselves; two things which I never knew you take the slightest concern in before."

Ross laughed and took her away, and Joanna, looking smilingly at Ellen, said—"Are you quite as much at a loss to understand all this as my mother, Ellen? Come, do exert yourself a little, and perhaps by and bye, with Mordaunt's assistance, you may find out the meaning of some of these extraordinary things." Ellen half laughed, and blushing, told her she was very teasing; but the pleasure which shone in her eyes evinced she was tolerably sure the cause of these new appearances, when explained, would not be disagreeable. Mrs. Ross came in again with a face of wonder, and saying only—"Lord bless me! well,—what strange things have come to pass!— come, Ellen, child, make haste and dress yourself as nicely as possible— come, Joanna, I want you—there are fifty things to do," took Joanna away. Ross joined Ellen, who was hastily putting up her work, impatient to escape to her own room, and reflect in quiet; and taking her hand with paternal tenderness, while his fine countenance was radiant with benevolent joy, said:—

"Compose yourself, my dear child; abate as much as possible this evident emotion; for though with pleasure I tell you every wish of your heart is likely to be fulfilled, nay in some respects perhaps exceeded, yet I would have you receive Mr. Mordaunt's declaration, of what I believe to be the sincerest regard, with something of composure, nay, even of dignity: for though, my dear girl, your station in life may, and does render you his inferior, yet, with your mind and person, he ought to think the affection of a heart so guileless no mean acquisition. Go, my dear, to your room, and tranquillize the too visible agitation of your spirits."

Ellen affectionately kissed the kind hand which held her own, and silently retired.

CHAP. IX.

——The sun goes down;
Far off his light is on the naked crags
Of Penmanmawr and Arvon's ancient hills;
And the last glory lingers yet awhile,
Crowning old Snowdon's venerable head,
That rose amid his mountains————
Where Mona the dark island stretch'd
Her shore along the ocean's lighter line.

SOUTHEY'S MADOR.

Pass we over the succeeding interview between Mordaunt and Ellen—its general style may be easily imagined; and the particulars of scenes like that seldom give pleasure, unless to those whom they immediately concern. It will be needless to specify that Ellen modestly, though frankly, confessed the influence he had obtained over her affections, and consented to be his wife: one, only one, painful objection arose in her mind—the probable distance she must be removed from her father, and the doubtfulness of her seeing him again, at least for years. These objections Mordaunt did his best to obviate, by reminding her that Powis was yet in a green old age, and would be well able to visit them; and that he would engage to revisit Llanwyllan with her, in the course of a year or two. Here, however, Mordaunt sighed deeply, and his countenance assumed that inexplicable gloom, with which reflexions on the past, or anticipations of the future, seemed always to inspire him: recovering himself a little, he added, "Remember, however, Ellen, this promise must be in some measure conditional. There are circumstances in my situation, which I have explained to Mr. Ross, which may affect my honour—almost strike at my life. Say, Ellen, can you willingly encounter those storms of adverse fate, which may assail, and, perhaps, make me an exile from my native country for ever? Can you give me so much of your confidence as to believe, whatever appearances may be, I am innocent?"

"Your words are full of mystery," said Ellen, in a faltering tone; "yet my heart is so fully convinced of your honour and veracity, that I can venture to promise no appearances shall ever shake my confidence in either—and if Mr. Ross knows those circumstances to which you allude, and yet is willing to join our hands, I have the best security that my heart has not misled my judgment."

"Admirable creature!" exclaimed Mordaunt: "how, in this sequestered situation, have you learnt so to temper the warmth of that innocent heart by the nicest rules of modesty and discrimination? How good you are, not to insist on my explaining all these mysteries!—Believe me, Ellen, I only postpone it in order to avoid as much as possible giving you pain. Perhaps, before any explanation becomes necessary, the clouds which have so long hovered over me may be dispersed. There is a clue, which (if the united efforts of myself and of the best of friends can attain it) will yet be found, that will unravel all that makes against me; and all will then be well." Here, for the present, the matter rested; and though to suppose Ellen void of curiosity would be to suppose her stupid, yet so entire was the confidence which she felt in Mordaunt's affection, and Ross's judgment, that she was perfectly satisfied to rest implicitly on them.

Mordaunt the next day made his application for Powis's consent to his marrying Ellen. His surprize at the proposal was such as evidently shewed it had never entered his imagination. After expressing his astonishment, he hesitated, and then replied: "Why, look ye, Mr. Mordaunt, you appear to be a gentleman, and I dare say have a good income. I can give Ellen a few hundreds now, and a few at my death; and I only want to be sure that you can maintain her in some sort of comfort.—You must tell me a little more of your situation in life; and though I like you very well, I should be glad to know from somebody who knows you what sort of a character you bear. Now don't be angry—I am a plain spoken man, and no more suspicious than another: but when you come and ask me for my only child, and to take her away, God knows where, into strange parts, I had need know whether you are likely to be kind to her."

Mordaunt seemed a little confused at this harangue; but replied: "You are very right, my good friend; I have already explained myself, my situation in life, and all circumstances, to Mr. Ross, who is of opinion I may marry your daughter, without doing her any injury in point of fortune—for your farther satisfaction, however, I refer you to the Rev. Doctor Montague, domestic chaplain to the Earl of St. Aubyn, at St. Aubyn Castle, Northamptonshire— his Lordship is at present not in England. That gentleman will give you every necessary detail respecting me; and should his account be satisfactory, I may then hope all obstacles are removed."

"You speak very handsomely, and like a gentleman, as I doubt not you are: but you will excuse my being a little anxious about my child—truth, to say, I do not like the notion of her going so far from me; but if she likes you (and I suppose you are pretty well agreed, or you would not come to me), I will never let my own comfort hinder her happiness; yet I tell you honestly, I had rather she had married Charles Ross, as I thought likely." At these words Mordaunt's countenance was overcast: he feared there had been some attachment between the young people; and such was the delicacy of his sentiments, that had he been certain of it, all his love for Ellen, passionate as it certainly was, would not have induced him to marry her; on this head, therefore, he was determined to be satisfied. He wrote Doctor Montague's address for Powis, and then went directly to the Parsonage, where Ellen still remained. He found her alone; and though he looked delighted to see her, she yet fancied she saw a little alteration in his manner, which disturbed her. He told her he had seen her father, and a part of what passed, omitting the mention of money concerns, which he thought would distress her.

When he was silent, she said: "Tell me, Mr. Mordaunt, am I mistaken in supposing you out of spirits to-day? I fear my father's rough manner has vexed you."—"No, Ellen, not that." "Then there is something, I am sure." "And do you already know me so well?" said Mordaunt. "I am ashamed to confess how unreasonable I am when you are so good and so confiding: but it is true—your father dropt a hint which alarmed me. He spoke of Charles Ross in terms that—forgive me, Ellen—that led me to fear, whatever might now be the case, he had not always been indifferent to you."

Ellen blushed a little, and said, with a calm smile, "It is certainly true, that Charles Ross professed a great attachment to me; and I believe his friends and my father earnestly wished we should at some time or other be married. Joanna, in particular, was very anxious, and has within a few months been quite uneasy on this subject, and indeed made me so too—for it was impossible——" She paused: then added, "I certainly felt the regard of a sister for Charles, but never more. If I had not—if you had never——" She hesitated, blushed, and said, with some warmth, "I never could have loved him enough to marry him."

Charmed, and with every suspicion laid at rest by this frank avowal, Mordaunt now was truly happy—for, till now, though hardly known to himself, a lurking doubt of Charles had at times hung about him. Mordaunt's former knowledge of the world had had the effect upon his heart, which it too often has, of repressing its confidence, and making it distrustful and suspicious. Great indeed had been his reasons for hardly believing the existence of real virtue, till he knew Ellen: her perfect innocence, her sweet simplicity, blended with the tenderest sensibility and acutest discernment, had once more restored his faith, and he now hoped and believed no future jealousies would cross his path. Yet surely he was venturing on doubtful ground. Great indeed must have been his risk in transplanting so fair a flower from the wildest part of Wales into the polished interior of England, and, probably, into a situation widely different from that she had hitherto filled! What could have implanted in the mind of a man so prone to jealousy as Mordaunt certainly was, so perfect a confidence in Ellen's veracity and virtue? It was, that he had observed in her an exalted, though not enthusiastic *piety*. Mordaunt, though a man of the world, was also a religious man; and in conversing, as he had done, frequently with Ellen on the subject of religion, he found her principles so fixed, and her mind so decidedly made up, and on such reasonable grounds, that he hesitated not in pronouncing her a Christian upon principle, and as such entitled to the firm confidence he felt in her sincerity and virtue.

Mordaunt now told her he should be absent all the next day, for it was necessary to write to one or two of his friends of the intended change in his prospects; and that, as he did not like to trust his letters to any common messenger, and indeed expected there were some of consequence lying for him at Carnarvon, he should go thither himself to fetch them; that as the distance was rather beyond what he liked to walk, especially now the days were so much shortened, he should borrow Ross's pony, and hoped to return in the evening. This scheme he executed accordingly; and Ross, understanding from Powis the mode proposed for his gaining farther intelligence of Mordaunt, thought, as Ellen was now returned to the Farm, it would be as well if Mordaunt absented himself in those little excursions he used so much to delight in, and restrained his visits to her in some degree, till her father's scruples were finally removed. To this, however, reluctantly they agreed; and Mordaunt accordingly spent the greatest part of the next week in viewing the face of the country, returning to his lodgings in the evening. Impatient of this vexatious restraint, Mordaunt, after three or four days, proposed to Ross and the girls an excursion to Snowdon, which, though he had seen, they had not, though living within ten or twelve miles of it. Mrs. Ross, who had of late greatly relaxed her vigilance respecting Ellen's industry, gave her consent; and mounted on their little Welsh ponies, the happy party set out with the day-break, a full moon promising to assist them on their return.

Leaving their horses at Dolbaden Castle, and taking guides with refreshments, each being armed with a spiked stick, they began the toilsome ascent. Ross, being fatigued, remained half way seated on an immense stone, till they should return. As they ascended the mountain, they perceived that its summit was covered with clouds, though, when they set out, it was perfectly clear, and the guides had assured them the day would be favourable. They now, however, began to apprehend that the thick clouds would prevent them from enjoying the reward of their labours, by depriving them of the view from the top of the mountain. The guides, notwithstanding, had still hopes that the day would ultimately clear up, and the event justified their expectations; for when within about half a mile of the summit, a fine breeze arose, and rolled the clouds like a curtain "down the steep of Snowdon's shaggy side," gradually disclosing its hollow apertures and broken precipices, with every variety of mountain, valley, lake, and stream; and below them, in every direction, a map of exquisite beauty, containing Carnarvon, the county of Chester, part of the North of England and Ireland, the Isle of Anglesea, and the Irish coast.

Here Mordaunt, sitting down with his fair companions, one on each side, on a low wall, which was probably built by shepherds for the safety of their flocks, but which now serves as a resting-place to travellers, expatiated with rapture on this amazingly sublime prospect. The "Bard" of Gray, and many of the beautiful passages of Mason's Elfrida and Caractacus were familiar to him; and these, with every grace of voice and action, he repeated, till the charmed and enthusiastic Ellen almost fancied she saw the white-robed druids with their crowns of mistletoe and golden harps pass in review before her. After having sufficiently rested, and taken some refreshment, they cautiously descended; and joining Ross, pursued the downward course of a mountain-stream of great beauty, which was frequently hurried over low rocks, forming numerous small but elegant cascades, till they reached the Castle, where they had left their ponies, and then returned by moonlight to Llanwyllan.

The next four or five days were employed in similar excursions. Not having been able on the day of their visit to Snowdon to extend their ride to Beth-gelert, their next object was to see the grave of the greyhound, and the romantic pass between Merioneth and Carnarvonshire, called Pont Aberglaslyn. At the grave of the greyhound Mordaunt repeated to his fair companions the interesting legend connected with it, and Spencer's elegant poem on the subject:—that little tale is so affecting, that, even at this remote period of time, no tender heart can hear it without lamenting the fate of the faithful and ill-requited Gelert. Ellen was not ashamed to drop a tear at the recital[1]. "Alas!" cried Mordaunt: "such is too frequently the fatal consequence of trusting to *appearances*! This excellent and unfortunate animal fell a sacrifice to circumstances, which, however apparently conclusive, were fallacious." He sighed, and fell for a few minutes into a gloomy silence, from which the soft voice of Ellen alone had power to rouse him.

They next visited Pont Aberglass-lyn, the wild and sublime scenery of which inspired them with awe. Its high grotesque rocks, surrounding like an amphitheatre the romantic bridge (consisting of a single arch thrown from one rough precipice to another), to which they approached by a road winding along a narrow stony valley, where the rocks on each side scarcely leave room for the road; and the dark impetuous stream, which rolls at the side of it, filled them with astonishment at the grandeur of the scene.

They visited also the little romantic village of Llanberis, with its beautiful vallies and lakes, surrounded by bold and prominent rocks, ascending almost abruptly from the edge of the water, and returned in the evening to Llanwyllan, delighted with an excursion which had afforded them so many beautiful views, and yet delightedly contrasting their own native village, with the dirty hovels, and miserable accommodations they had met with in their progress; for the exertions of Ross and his wife, who were both English, and had in the early part of their lives resided wholly in England, had introduced a degree of neatness and comfort both in the houses and apparel of their parishioners, which gave Llanwyllan the appearance of a comfortable English village, and rendered it totally distinct from those near it; where, as is often the case in Wales, extreme poverty, and its too frequent concomitants, a total carelessness of comfort abound.

They also visited Carnarvon, which the girls found much altered since they had seen it some years before, and were quite surprized at the carriages, and smartly drest people in the streets. Of course they went to the Castle, and saw the chamber where, it is said, the weak and unfortunate Edward II. was born; though that fact, from the meanness of its appearance, and inconvenient situation, appears extremeful doubtful, if not improbable. In short, they seemed in a new world, so very different were the scenes around them from those to which they were accustomed.

"Ah, Ellen!" said Joanna, "all this will soon be as nothing to you: you will see so many fine houses and great cities, you will wonder how you could ever fancy Carnarvon a large place: and I shall remain in our little quiet village, which, when you are gone, I shall think stupid, and never go beyond it!"— "Do not think so," replied Ellen: "I hope, if indeed I do leave Llanwyllan (for I consider nothing settled till Mr. Montague's letter arrives), I hope it will not be long before I shall have you with me—it will be one of my first wishes as soon as I find myself at all accustomed to the change In my situation." Joanna seemed much delighted with this promise; they slept that night at Carnarvon, and returned the next day to Llanwyllan.

In the course of these journies much conversation took place between Mordaunt and Ellen; but he with great generosity forbore as much as possible from all particular topics, as he wished to leave her as much unfettered as was now in his power till the arrival of Montague's letter; for though he had no doubt of what the contents would be, yet till he had obtained Powis's free consent, he could not exactly consider her as his affianced bride; but for conversation they were never at a loss—literary subjects furnished them with an inexhaustible fund of delight; for Mordaunt's mind and memory were so well stored with poetical and classical treasures, he scarcely needed books of reference; the beautiful views which they also obtained of the heavenly bodies, in their mountainous excursions, inspired Ellen with a desire to know something of astronomy, and Mordaunt was thoroughly capable of being her instructor. In this Ross assisted him; and two hours in the latter part of the evening were sweetly past in this delightful study. Mordaunt was also, though not a finished artist, yet very capable of taking sketches from the surrounding country; and already Ellen began to use her pencil also in slight attempts, which he both encouraged and directed—so happy indeed was the life they now led, that the slight restraint thrown upon their feelings seemed rather to give a zest to their meetings than to destroy their pleasure: gladly, most gladly, would both have relinquished all change of station, and remained for the rest of their lives in the peaceful shades of Llanwyllan.

——What was the world to them?
Its pomp, its pleasure, and its nonsense all?
Who, in each other, saw whatever fair,
High fancy forms, or lavish hearts can wish:
Something than beauty dearer, should they look;
Or on the mind, or mind illumined face,
Truth, goodness, honour, harmony, and love,
The richest bounty of indulgent Heaven.

CHAP. X.

Now go with me, and with this holy man,
Into the chantry by; there, before him,
And underneath that consecrated roof,
Plight me the full assurance of your faith.

TWELFTH NIGHT.

At length, for in this remote village letters were not speedily exchanged, the answer from Doctor Montague arrived: it contained the following lines.

> Sir,
>
> I receive Mr. Mordaunt's reference to me as a favour, and hasten to reply to your's of the 5th inst. by saying that I have had the happiness of knowing that gentleman from his youth, and am entirely convinced of his being a man of the most perfectly honourable and excellent character. As you have been obliging enough to account for this application, I can only add that your daughter will in my opinion have reason to esteem herself the most fortunate of women in becoming his wife. Mr. Mordaunt's fortune is sufficiently ample to enable him to live with perfect ease and comfort.
>
> I am, Sir,
> With great respect,
> Your's, obediently,
> GEORGE MONTAGUE.
>
> St. Aubyn Castle,
> Sep. 18th, 18—.

Nothing could be more satisfactory than this honourable testimony to the good qualities of Mr. Mordaunt; and Powis began to feel half ashamed of having doubted for an instant the honour of a man so highly estimated: he hastened with the letter in his hand to Ellen, who, with Joanna for her inmate, was now at home, and exclaiming, "There, child, read that," gave her the letter: the emotions of his affectionate heart, bursting out from time to time while she was reading it, in words pronounced at intervals, and with some difficulty, such as, "Well!—so I must lose her—the pride of my life! but she will be happy I hope, dear soul! This seems to be a man of some consequence: why, she will be quite a lady; not above her old friends, though, I hope, Joanna!"

When Ellen had finished the letter, she rose, and throwing herself into her father's arms, wept with mingled emotions of sorrow and gladness; for sincerely as she rejoiced in such a character of her beloved Mordaunt, she greatly regretted the certainty that if she married him, she must immediately leave her father. Powis's heart was melted by the same consideration, and the tears running down his rough face fell on Ellen's bosom: at last she articulated, "Oh, my dear father, I cannot leave you!" Powis, half sobbing half smiling, said, "Why indeed, my child, I know not how to bear the thoughts of parting from you, but if not *now*, I must some time or other; and I will not prepare a pain for my death-bed so terrible as that would be which should tell me I had preferred my own selfish happiness to thine." At this tender, this affecting thought, the tears of Ellen redoubled, and Joanna's accompanied them. Just then Mordaunt, who had seen the boy who brought letters to Llanwyllan, pass towards the farm, came in impatient to know if Montague's answer had arrived: he was surprized and almost alarmed at the scene before him. Powis lifted up his head, and rubbing his eyes, said, "I am ashamed of myself to be such a child!—here, Mr. Mordaunt, is your friend's letter, and here, if you will accept of her, is your wife." He disengaged himself from Ellen's clasping arms, and gently placed her in those which Mordaunt eagerly extended to receive her.

All was now soon settled; for Powis, though an unlearned was not an unwise man; and seeing the necessity of Mordaunt's return to his own abode before the season changed, he would not suffer any selfish considerations of his own comfort to divide the lovers during a dreary winter, which would now quickly overtake them. He left every thing respecting money matters to Mr. Ross. Mordaunt gave that gentleman a bond, expressed in such terms as fully convinced him Ellen's pecuniary concerns would be amply considered; and generously refused to accept of any money with his bride, gaily telling Powis, that now he was robbed of his daughter, he hoped he would look out for a wife himself, and retain Ellen's intended portion to encrease his future means of ease and comfort; or, that if he really did not know what to do with the money, he should give it to Joanna when she married. "Well," said Powis, "you are either very rich or very proud, Mr. Mordaunt." "I shall be both when Ellen is my wife," answered Mordaunt.

Mordaunt requested that Ellen would furnish herself with no more cloaths on the occasion than were absolutely necessary, till they should reach Bristol: "Where," he said, "I hope, my dear girl, to find some fashionable mantua-maker, who will at least give you a more modern wardrobe than you could meet with here." "You are determined, I see," said Ellen, "that I shall be obliged to no one but yourself." "For Heaven's sake, Ellen!" replied

Mordaunt, hastily, "do not talk of such a paltry concern as a few cloaths, as an obligation: how shall I ever repay those I owe to your confidence and kindness?"

Few were the preparations requisite for the marriage of Mordaunt and Ellen. He with some difficulty procured a chaise from Carnarvon on the morning of their marriage, for the roads between that place and Llanwyllan were in some parts almost impassable for a carriage, and had not the autumn been uncommonly fine and dry, would have been entirely so. On the third of October, at a very early hour, the little party met at Powis's house, and from thence proceeded to the village church, where, from her father's hand, Mordaunt received his lovely bride. Mr. Ross performed the ceremony, and at the end of it added an extempore and most eloquent prayer for the happiness of friends so dear to him, with a fervency of devotion that drew tears into every eye. When all the party had quitted the vestry, after having registered the marriage of Constantine Frederick Mordaunt and Ellen Powis, Ross and Mordaunt stepped back an instant, as if something had been forgotten: as they returned, Ellen heard Ross say, "I rely implicitly upon it, and let me beg it may be done as soon as possible." "Depend upon my sacred honour," answered Mordaunt, impressively: "or, if you wish it, on my most solemn oath." "It needs not that," said Ross; "I am satisfied." "Then so am I," thought Ellen, "for strange as such frequent mysteries appear, Ross, I am sure, would never partake of one, which was not perfectly innocent."

Let us not attempt to describe the parting of Powis and his daughter, which took place an hour after the marriage ceremony was concluded. Mordaunt repeated his assurances of returning, if possible, to Llanwyllan the following summer; then almost by force severing Ellen from her father, he placed her in the chaise, and, following hastily, bowed his farewell. The motion of the carriage, to which she was wholly unused, roused Ellen from the half-fainting into which she had fallen, and the tender soothings of Mordaunt at length revived and composed her. As they passed on, the varied face of the country, the beautiful and extensive scenery through which they journied, awakened all the soft enthusiasm of her youthful mind, which, shaking off the dejection caused by parting from her first connections, roused itself to the perception of the happy prospects the future might present.

"And thou, oh! Hope, with eyes so fair,
What was thy delighted measure?
Still it whispered promised pleasure,
And bade the lovely scenes at distance hail."

After several days travelling, stopping occasionally to rest, and to view such remarkable objects as they thought worthy of observation, they arrived at the

Passage, and, crossing it, soon after entered the city of Bristol. To paint Ellen's surprise at all the wonders of the new world which surrounded her would be impossible; so strange indeed did every thing appear to her, that scarcely the influence which Mordaunt possessed over her mind could prevent her from exclamations of astonishment, which, to those around, would have betrayed the perfect seclusion in which she had hitherto lived. After shewing her all that was worth notice in Bristol and its interesting environs, Mordaunt took his fair bride to Bath, with the elegance of which she was particularly delighted. The streets, the shops, were a constant source of amusement to one so new to every thing; here, however, they remained but three days, during which Mordaunt procured for Ellen such a variety of dresses as appeared to her quite extraordinary; and she began to think her husband was either very rich or very extravagant, though in truth all he purchased would hardly satisfy the "indispensable necessities" of most *young ladies*, of no pretensions really higher than those of Ellen Powis had been; and were far from appearing to Mordaunt more than barely sufficient for her present occasions. An elegant new riding habit and hat were amongst them; and Ellen's delicate figure appeared to such advantage in that dress, that no one could have supposed her so lately removed from so remote a situation: her natural gracefulness prevented her appearing in the slightest degree awkward; and her new dress gave her an air of fashion, with which Mordaunt was delighted.

From Bath they went to London, where Mordaunt engaged very handsome lodgings, though not in the most fashionable part of the town, yet in a handsome street, for a fortnight, where they rested after the fatigues of so long a journey. Mordaunt told his wife he wished not to take her to any of the public amusements till the next spring, when he hoped to revisit London with her, and when some ladies of his acquaintance would be there also, and would accompany her. Ellen, who desired no greater pleasure than his society, was well contented with this arrangement: during their stay in London, therefore, they seldom went out; but Mordaunt trusted her two or three times under the care of the person at whose house they lodged, (who was a very respectable woman) to go to different shops, furnishing her liberally with money, and insisting on her providing a very complete and elegant wardrobe. Several times Ellen wished to check his liberality, assuring him she had already as much of every thing as she wished for; but he replied she was no judge of what she would want when she went into the country, and that she must oblige him by buying every thing in abundance, and of the best and most fashionable materials; nor did he ever go from home without bringing back with him some elegant trinket or set of ornaments for her; so that little as she was a judge of the value of money, she was surprized and somewhat uneasy to see Mordaunt so profuse of his, for in addition to the large expences he would incur in her dress, he had requested Mrs. Birtley (the person at whose house they lodged) to hire a young woman to wait upon his wife; and Ellen really thought her new servant so much more like a lady than till very lately she had thought herself, that she hardly knew how to give her any orders. Mordaunt had also hired a job chariot and horses for the time they staid in town.

Their landlady observing the extreme youth and simplicity of Ellen, contrasted by that air of the world and of fashion so conspicuous in Mordaunt, as well as that though he hardly appeared to endure her being out of his sight, he seldom went abroad with her, and that they seemed to have no friends or connections in London, began to form conjectures not very much to the advantage of her guests; and as she was a woman of good character, though of somewhat a suspicious turn, she was not sorry when they left her apartments.

Mordaunt chose not to take Jane, Ellen's new maid, with them, but left directions for her to travel by the stage to the town which was nearest to his residence in Northamptonshire, where she should be met by a servant, who would conduct her to his house.

For the first day of their journey Mordaunt appeared at times in deep reflection, and as if revolving in his mind a variety of considerations, frequently catching Ellen's hand in his own, he would express the rapture he felt in the certainty of possessing her affection, and that she was securely his; then he would add, "Remember, Ellen, you have promised to take me *for better for worse*: tell me, do you think any change in my situation could impair your love for me?" To these questions she returned such tender and affectionate answers, as seemed for the time to dispel from his mind every uneasy sensation; yet still at intervals his thoughtfulness returned, and began at last to inspire Ellen with a sort of anxiety she could not wholly overcome.

The next day Mordaunt proposed resting a few hours at a pleasant village, which he told her was only about twenty miles from his own house, but that he thought it would be more agreeable to her not to arrive at home till towards the evening: to this she readily consented; it was indeed very agreeable to her, but had it been less so, she knew no will but his.

After breakfast, the landlady of the inn where they had taken that meal, coming in, Mordaunt asked her how far it was from thence to St. Aubyn Castle; she answered about nineteen miles: after asking her some more questions respecting the length of the stages, &c. he inquired if she knew Lord St. Aubyn; she replied she had seen his Lordship once before he went abroad, but she heard he was now soon expected home again; a gentleman who stopped at her house not many days before, told her his Lordship was lately returned from Spain, and was coming very shortly to the Castle. On being asked if she knew who that gentleman was, she said it was the Reverend

Doctor Montague, his Lordship's domestic Chaplain. Mordaunt then asked her if Lord St. Aubyn was much liked in his neighbourhood, and she gave him a very high character for his charity to the poor, and kindness to his servants and dependants.

Ellen here whispered to her husband that she would inquire what sort of a character *one Mr. Mordaunt*, his Lordship's steward, bore. Mordaunt laughed, and said she was very malicious, and only hoped to hear some evil of him. She then repeated her question, looking playfully at him, to which the landlady replied, that she did not know Mr. Mordaunt except by name, but she heard he was a very worthy old gentleman. The idea of Mordaunt's being called an *old gentleman* diverted Ellen so much, that she burst into a laugh she could not repress, in which Mordaunt joined so heartily, as half offended the good woman, who, supposing she had committed some blunder, left the room immediately.

"Come, my dear Ellen," said Mordaunt, when he had composed his features, "let us take a walk through this pleasant village: it is long since you enjoyed the pure air of the country." "Indeed, my dear *old gentleman*," Ellen gaily replied, "I shall be very glad to find myself once more at liberty to walk a little, for I began to feel tired of the restraint of a carriage, which, when we left Llanwyllan, I thought so delightful, I could never be weary of it."

CHAP. XI.

You see me, Lord Bassanio, where I stand,
Such as I am; though for myself alone
I would not be ambitious in my wish,
To wish myself much better, yet for you
I would be trebled twenty times myself,
A thousand times more fair, ten thousand times
More rich————but the full sum of me
Is an unlessoned girl, unschooled, unpractised;
Happy in this, she is not yet so old
But she may learn; and happier than this,
She is not bred so dull but she can learn;
Happiest of all, is that her gentle spirit
Commits herself to your's to be directed.

MERCHANT OF VENICE.

───────────────────────

After strolling through some very pleasant fields, they came to a sequestered spot, where tall trees shaded a little murmuring rivulet, near whose banks a very neat farm-house attracted their attention.

"Ah, this reminds me of dear Llanwyllan!" said Ellen: "how much I should like to sit down here awhile!" "That," answered Mordaunt, "may be easily effected." He then went to the door, where he met a nice looking elderly woman, the farmer's wife, and saying he was thirsty, asked her to spare him a draught of milk or whey, with which she very civilly complied, and requested them to walk in. Ellen, delighted with the sight of the farm-yard and smell of the dairy, readily consented, and at Mordaunt's desire, the good woman said she would give them some cream, bread, &c. With great civility therefore, she shewed them into a neat parlour, and having placed before them brown bread, cream, and some bunches of well-ripened grapes, left them to themselves.

Ellen said:—"Now, my dear Mordaunt, I really feel as if I were at home again, and can *do the honours* (as you term it) of this little table very tolerably; but if, as I suspect, you are much visited by high people near you, will you not often have to blush for your awkward little rustic?" "If I had feared that," answered Mordaunt, "I would not have ventured it; but, as I have often told you, the natural propriety of your manner will very well supply the place of artificial graces; and as to the mere forms of society, they are so easily acquired, you will speedily attain them: but tell me, Ellen, after the cursory view you have had of something more refined, could you now be contented to sit down here for the rest of your life?" "With you," replied the tender Ellen, "I could be not only contented but happy any where yet I own *you* seem to me formed for something so superior, that I should forever regret your being confined to a sphere so limited."

Mordaunt, delighted with the sweetness of her words and manners, scarcely knew how to express how greatly he was pleased with all she said. After a few minutes he opened the little casement, for the day was mild and clear, more like spring than the beginning of November; and gathering some late blossoms of a white jassamine, which grew round it, and in that sheltered spot, so soft had been the season, still retained their beauty: he twisted them with some very small vine leaves across her brow, amongst her fine hair, in a very particular style, and making her look in the little glass which hung in the room where they sat, he said:—

"There, Ellen, *that* is very like a countess's coronet; the jasmine may pass for pearls, and the little branch of the vine for strawberry leaves: how should you like one in pearls or diamonds? I think it becomes you inimitably well." "This simple wreath may," she said, smiling as she surveyed herself; "but I believe that this little rustic person would not assort very well with the splendid ornament you describe." He smiled, and said—"Do not take it off, but sit down, and I will tell you a story." "A story!—delightful! I hope it is entertaining." "Very, and perfectly true. *Once upon a time*: do you like that beginning?" "Not much; it is too childish: try again." "Well then, once in the days of King Arthur——" "Oh! do not go quite so far back—your story will last all day." "What! a Welsh girl and not like to hear a tale of King Arthur. Oh! most degenerate damsel." Ellen still laughing, said—"Come, dear Mordaunt, make haste, I long to hear this interesting story."

He placed himself at her side, and with some agitation, said:—

"Ellen, the time is come to clear up some of the mysterious words you have heard me utter at Llanwyllan: what will you say to me when I tell you—yet be not alarmed—when I tell you that, though my *name* is really *Mordaunt*, yet I have *deceived* you—for that is not my *only* designation: do not look so surprised and bewildered, my love; I am not *inferior* to the man you suppose me: he is indeed my relation, being the natural son of my father's brother: he is many years older than I am. Tell me, Ellen, are you afraid to hear the rest?" "No," she replied firmly, though with marks of the most impatient curiosity in her countenance. "I am so convinced of your integrity, that be who or what you will, I am happy in being your wife, and ready to share your station, be it ever so lowly." "Enchanting creature!" he exclaimed, and clasped her to his bosom: "know then, that were the coronet which binds your brow of the most costly materials instead of a simple flower, it is your's by right, for I am the Earl, and you are the Countess of St. Aubyn."

A moment Ellen struggled with the overwhelming surprize: then said: "How could you condescend to one so much beneath you?" "Beneath me!" he replied—"oh, in every thing but the mere accident of birth how greatly my superior! But the surprize, my gentle love, has made you a little pale; recover yourself, and let me see you again gay and playful as when you supposed yourself only Mrs. Mordaunt." He fixed his penetrating eyes upon her: even in that tender moment he sought to discover if any undue pride or vanity elated her; but there was no trace of any such ignoble passion: surprized, astonished as she was, and feeling some diminution of the ease and equality with which she had but lately learned to regard him, Ellen more than half regretted to find him so greatly her superior, and to see herself raised so very much beyond the station her humility led her to believe the only one she could fill with propriety; yet she must have been more or less than woman, had she not felt charmed with the disinterested love St. Aubyn had evinced in making her his wife.

Having a little recovered the emotion this interesting discovery had caused in both, Ellen entreated him, whom yet she hardly knew how to name, to explain the reason of his having appeared at Llanwyllan in a character so inferior to his own; which he did in these words:

"I cannot, my love, nor would I wish at present to tell you all my story, though some day you shall know every circumstance of my life: may they come to your knowledge without lessening your felicity!" He sighed, and thus continued:—"Some domestic misfortunes induced me, at different times, to make several excursions under the name I bore when first I met you, which is, indeed, that of my family: since my last return from the Continent, about six months ago, I did not let my friends or servants know I was come to England, but set out to travel through Wales, sometimes by one mode of conveyance, sometimes another, and not unfrequently as a mere pedestrian. I was always a good walker, and had been accustomed to pass whole days on foot amongst the mountains of Spain; frequently, therefore, I preferred walking, as giving me better opportunities of exploring the most romantic scenes. In one of these excursions I found myself at Llanwyllan; there I merely intended to stay a day or two, till accident, and your father's hospitality, introduced you to my knowledge—need I relate to you the progress of that passion which soon took possession of my heart, and left me powerless to quit you. A very few days determined me, if your affections were disengaged, to do all in my power to secure your love; yet I delayed the declaration of my own, in hopes of bringing some untoward circumstances to a favourable conclusion; but when I found our good friend Ross began to be alarmed for you, and fancied I saw in my Ellen's sweet face that she was not happy, I thought it necessary to come to some decision, and to Ross I fully explained my *whole* situation: he was so perfectly convinced of my honour and integrity, that he consented to give his lovely pupil to me, even under all the unpleasant circumstances which at present embarrass and torment me; and even though we both doubted whether a marriage contracted by me under the name of Mordaunt only would be completely binding: to obviate this objection, I bound myself to him, not only to make upon you such settlements as my large income rendered proper, and my heart prompted, but to remarry you as soon as I could do so without absolute impropriety; and that I will do if I live before I sleep again; though I believe the precautions we took render it unnecessary, for after you left the vestry, the day we were married, Ross and myself, as perhaps you observed, returned, and in his presence I added the title of Earl of St. Aubyn to the names of Constantine Frederick Mordaunt, which, I have no doubt, would substantiate our marriage in any court in England: to avoid, however, all possible doubt, now or in future, on this important point, I have at this instant a special licence in my possession, and this evening, at Castle St. Aubyn, Montague shall read the marriage service to us again.—Are you satisfied with this arrangement, my love?"

"I am so ignorant in every thing, that I can only rely on you; which I do implicitly, and with full confidence."

Ellen then asked St. Aubyn if Doctor Montague knew who he was in reality recommending to her father, or whether he supposed it to be indeed Mr. Mordaunt? Lord St. Aubyn laughed at this question, and said Montague would have had reason to be surprized at hearing Mordaunt was going to be married, as he was a very stiff old Bachelor of at least sixty; but the fact was, he had written himself to Montague from Llanwyllan, informing him who the person really was respecting whom Powis's inquiries would be made, and desiring him to give such a character of *that person* as he thought was deserved, only not to betray his real title, as he was anxious to avoid the *eclat* such a discovery would produce, if made while they remained at Llanwyllan.

After a little more conversation on this interesting subject, St. Aubyn and his Ellen took leave of their hospitable entertainer, after remunerating her in the most liberal way for the trouble they had given her; and as by the time they reached the village the day was far advanced, they ordered a chaise directly, and proceeded to the end of the next stage, where they dined, and where St. Aubyn told Ellen his own carriage was to meet them, and convey them to the Castle, where his household were instructed to expect their lady.

Before they had quite dined, an elegant new travelling carriage and four, with coronets on the pannels, and out-riders in rich liveries, drove to the door, and the host, who had no idea of the rank of his guests, from their arriving in a hack carriage, unattended, was in the act of denying to the servants that Lord and Lady St. Aubyn were there, when the Earl, throwing up the sash, told the men to move about, but not put up the horses, as he should go in half an hour. While he was speaking, the stage-coach from London stopt at the door, and Ellen's maid stepping out, inquired whether any servant from one Mr. Mordaunt's, in that neighbourhood, was waiting for her. St. Aubyn, calling to one of his men, desired him to send that young woman to Lady St. Aubyn. The man obeyed, and told the astonished Jane she must go and speak to his lady. "What for, pray?" answered Jane, pertly. "Indeed I shall do no such thing; I am going on directly, and don't want such fellows as you to be joking with me." "Jane!" said Ellen, approaching the window, anxious to put a stop to a dialogue she feared might disclose more than she wished the servants should know. "Oh, dear Ma'am, are you there!" answered Jane. "Oh! I am so glad; I will come to you, Ma'am, directly." One of the men, wishing for an opportunity of seeing his new lady, said, "Come, young woman, I will shew you the way to her Ladyship."

The poor girl was so much confused, by these different directions, that fortunately she had no power to refuse, or indeed to speak at all, but followed the servant into the room, where St. Aubyn and Ellen were sitting. "There," said the footman, in a low voice, and giving her a little push: "go in, child— that is my lady." "Grant me patience," said Jane, turning sharply to him: "why I tell you that is *my* mistress. I suppose you want to persuade me I don't know my own———." "Softly, Jane," said St. Aubyn: "there, go in, and speak to your lady, and you, Thomas, may go; we shall soon be ready to start."

He left Jane with her lady, not wishing to be present at the explanation. Ellen explained to the astonished girl, that she had, for particular reasons, concealed her title while in London, and did not wish her to say to the other servants that she had ever known her under any other name. Jane very willingly promised obedience, and was not a little elated to find herself own woman to Lady St. Aubyn, instead of waiting-maid to plain Mrs. Mordaunt. Indeed, Mrs. Birtley had had some scruples about suffering her to follow the mysterious couple at all, and charged her, if she did not find all right, to leave her place, and return to London immediately, all which her unguarded hints betrayed to Ellen, who felt a little confused at hearing her situation had been so misconstrued. "And there, Ma'am—beg pardon—my lady—there your Ladyship;" (for Jane was willing to make amends for her former ignorance, by using Ellen's title as often as possible)—"there your Ladyship left a book at Mrs. Birtley's—I forget the name of it; some poetry book it was, and in it was written, in one place, 'C. F. M. to Ellen P.' and I was to have brought it with me, but Mrs. Birtley was not at home when I came away, so I could not have it, and it was a great pity, for it is very handsome, in a fine binding, and with beautiful pictures: one of them was a man jumping off a rock, like into the sea, and with a sort of a clergyman's gown on, and with a musical instrument in his hand, something like a guitar, but not quite." "I know the book you mean," said Ellen; "it was Gray's Poems. I am sorry I left it behind." "Yes, Ma'am—my lady I mean, that was the very book; but I dare say your Ladyship can have it by sending to Mrs. Birtley; and in one part, my lady, there was a print of a church-yard, and over the print was put, 'Dear Landwilliam,' or some such name." "Yes, Jane, yes; that's the book—that will do: now give me my hat, and step down and inquire if Lord St. Aubyn is waiting for me."

It was the first time Ellen had framed her lips to say Lord St. Aubyn, and she wondered whether she should ever become accustomed to the sound. Jane was met at the door by one of the men servants, who came to know if her lady was ready, as his lord bade him say the carriage was come round. Jane, astonished at her own greatness, in being called Ma'am, and so respectfully addressed by such a fine gentleman, returned to Ellen with redoubled respect, and a new reinforcement of "my ladies." Ellen said she was ready, and ran down. "Come, my love," said St. Aubyn, "we shall be late at home."

Ellen's heart throbbed, as she thought of a home so far above her utmost ideas of splendour, and of being called to a situation to which she feared herself unequal; yet she composed her spirits as well as she could; for she saw, that to please her lord she must assert herself, and behave with a degree of dignity and self possession: she gave him her hand, therefore, with tenderness, but with a certain air of calmness, as if not too much elated with her new honours, or childishly delighted with her new carriage: he saw, and was charmed with her just discrimination, and encouraged her by saying, "Ever, my Ellen, all I wish." He then placed her in the carriage, and leaving Jane to follow with the luggage in a hack chaise, they were speedily on the road to Castle St. Aubyn. As they drew near it, they passed a neat little mansion, standing on a small lawn, surrounded by flowering shrubs, which St. Aubyn told Ellen was the house of the *real* Mr. Mordaunt. "Exactly such a place," said she, "had I figured to myself as your habitation, not indeed in Wales, for there my imagination did not soar to a pitch so high; but since we have been in England, and I saw what the smaller houses of genteel people were, such I fancied your's." "In a few minutes, my love," he replied, "we shall approach my real home, and most happy am I to say, my Ellen's home also; though in a different style, it will, I hope, be as much to your taste as this pretty place appears to be."

As he spoke, one of the out-riders passed the carriage, and ringing at a porter's lodge, the large and elegant iron gates were thrown open, and they turned into a noble park of no common dimensions. Here the hand of art had followed, not impeded that of nature: large trees, disposed in clumps, or singly, as the purest taste directed, shaded and ornamented the verdant lawn. A fine piece of water, almost bearing the aspect of a fine lake, with an elegant pleasure barge at anchor on its bank, skirted one side of the road which led to the house. Its pure waters were enlivened by various aquatic fowls, and on the shelving edges were light and tasteful cages for gold and silver pheasants and other foreign birds; while in picturesque groups under the trees, or bounding away at the approach of the carriage, herds of the finest deer gave new animation to the scene.

Ellen, enchanted, enraptured, though the closing twilight hardly afforded her light sufficient to see half the beauties round her, was every moment uttering exclamations of delight, with which St. Aubyn was highly gratified: but as they approached the immense pile of building which he told her was the house, she gradually assumed a more composed demeanor, determined not to betray to the servants that such things were totally new to her.

CHAP. XII.

A happy rural seat of various view,
Groves whose rich trees wept od'rous gums and balm.———
Betwixt them lawns, or level downs and flocks
Grazing the tender herb, were interspersed;
Or palmy hillock, or the flow'ry lap,
Of some irriguous valley spread her store,
Flow'rs of all hue.———
Meanwhile murmuring waters fall
Down the slope hills, dispersed; or in a lake———
Unite their streams—
The birds their choirs apply, airs, vernal airs,
Breathing the smell of field and grove attune,
The trembling leaves———

PARADISE LOST.

A train of servants in the spacious hall stood ready to receive their Lord and Lady. Amongst them was a respectable middle-aged woman, who, with deep respect, mingled with tears of joy and affection, addressed the Earl: he kindly and condescendingly took her hand, and said, "My good Mrs. Bayfield, I hope you are quite well: I am rejoiced to see you look so. See, my worthy friend, I have brought you a new Lady. Ellen, my love, I am sure I need not tell you to esteem my good housekeeper and nurse, for such she has been to me in much of illness and affliction." Ellen, with some kind words, offered her hand to Mrs. Bayfield, who, courtesying, received it with an air of the most profound respect. St. Aubyn also spoke with great kindness to the other servants, and then led Ellen into a magnificent library, which he told her was his usual sitting-room when at St. Aubyn's. Ellen, fatigued with her journey and the surprizing occurrences of the day, was not then able to do more than take a cursory survey of it; but she saw that here was entertainment and instruction enough to fill a long life, if even wholly devoted to literary pursuits.

In a few minutes a man of a venerable appearance, dressed in the cassock of a dignified clergyman, entered the library, whom St. Aubyn announced to Ellen as his friend and chaplain the Rev. Doctor Montague. "See, my dear Montague," said he, "this lovely creature, who has generously forgiven my appearing to her in an assumed character, and before she knew how much my real station was superior to that in which she first saw me, most kindly assured me of her perfect willingness to share my fate, be it what it might."

He gave her hand to the good old man, who, clasping it between both his, said, "Pardon, Madam, this freedom in a man who has for many years felt the affection of a father for your excellent Lord." Ellen bent her knee to him as to a second Ross, whose blessing she had been accustomed to ask in that posture with Joanna. The venerable man understood the graceful appeal, although fashion has so long proscribed it to her votaries; and raising his hands and eyes, said, "God bless you, lovely lady, and you, my dear Lord, with her!"

St. Aubyn then said a few words in a low voice to the Doctor, to which he replied, "Certainly, my Lord: if you have the least doubt of the entire legality of your marriage, it will be far the best way: have you the licence?" "Yes, here," said the Earl: "examine it, if you please. Ellen, my love," he added, turning towards her, "are your spirits too much fatigued, or will you oblige me, by allowing Montague to read the marriage-ceremony to us: I have a special licence from the Archbishop, and it will not take many minutes?" Ellen bowed a silent assent; and Montague, saying it would be proper to have witnesses, proposed speaking to Mrs. Bayfield, and Thornton, Lord St. Aubyn's gentleman, on whose secrecy they might rely, as of course it was desirable not to have the transaction made public. He went therefore to them, and having told them all that was necessary, they immediately attended; and the marriage-ceremony being read, Montague prepared a certificate, which was signed by all present, and deposited in Ellen's care.

All parties seemed rejoiced when this embarrassing business was concluded, which though it gratified Ellen as shewing her Lord's extreme anxiety to satisfy any doubt she might feel, yet could not be agreeable to either. A Sandwich tray was soon after brought in, filled with refreshments: after partaking of which, Ellen and the wondering Jane were shewn to an elegant dressing-room, which communicated with a still more splendid bed-chamber, both fitted up with the most peculiar attention, not only to costliness and effect, but to convenience and comfort, as the contrivances for hot and cold baths, and every luxurious accommodation both here and in a gentleman's dressing-room on the other side the bed-room, sufficiently evinced. All Jane's profound respect for her Lady could not keep her entirely silent, nor repress the exclamations of wonder and delight with which she greeted every elegant article of furniture: above all, a rich service of dressing-plate on the toilette attracted her attention. "How beautiful, how costly! And here again, what fine glasses! Dear, my Lady, you may see yourself from head to foot; and so clear, they make you look, if possible, more beautiful than you really are!"

Ellen, nearly as little acquainted with such objects as her maid, was not sorry to have only this simple girl witness to her actions, which would have betrayed to a more practised observer that she herself hardly knew the use of half the splendid articles before her. She endeavoured, however, to assume a graver manner, and to keep Jane at a greater distance; but the good-natured creature mixed so much affectionate respect with her somewhat too familiar prattle, Ellen could not be angry with her: she dismissed her, however, as soon as possible, with a reiterated caution not to betray to the servants that she had ever known her under any other name than that she bore at present.

The next day Ellen took a nearer survey of her noble habitation: the height and size of the rooms, the splendid furniture, and rich decorations, absolutely bewildered her senses; and when in an immense mirror, which hung at one end of a superb drawing-room, she saw herself reflected from head to foot, she, like the innocent Zilia[2], actually fancied for a moment it was some elegant female coming to meet her.

Passing through this room, she entered one smaller, indeed, but fitted up with such exquisite taste, as quite enchanted her: the furniture and hangings were of pale green silk, lightly ornamented with gold; the ground of the carpet, pale green, worked with the needle in bunches of the most beautiful natural flowers, which really appeared to be growing there. The tables, chairs, candelabras, and every article of furniture, were formed after the antique, and caught the eye of Ellen by the perfection of their figures and disposition; so true it is, that what is really beautiful and in perfect taste will please the unpractised as well as the critical observer, provided the natural taste has not been vitiated by any false ideas of proportion and ornament.

On the Countess's expressing herself particularly pleased with this room, Mrs. Bayfield (who had undertaken to shew her the house, for St. Aubyn had been interrupted in his intention of doing so by Mr. Mordaunt, who brought him some papers of consequence to inspect), looking cautiously round, said, "If your Ladyship pleases, it will be better not to tell my Lord that you like this room in particular." "Why so, Mrs. Bayfield?" asked Ellen, struck with surprize at this request, and the manner it was made in. "Why, Madam," replied Mrs. Bayfield, "this room and the small one within were fitted up by my late Lady according to her own fancy, and were always called her drawing-room and boudoir; and since her death, my Lord has never liked the rooms." "Lady St. Aubyn then has not been dead long, I suppose," said Ellen; "for the furniture of these rooms appears almost new." "About seven years, Madam; but the rooms have scarcely ever been used: they were furnished not long before she went abroad with my Lord." "Was this beautiful carpet her own work?" asked Ellen. "Oh dear, no, Madam! my late Lady was of too gay a turn to do such a piece of work: it was my Lord's *mother* worked this."

"I thought you had meant your Lord's mother, Mrs. Bayfield: who then do you call your late Lady?" "My Lord's first wife, Madam, the late Countess of St. Aubyn."

"The *late* Countess—my Lord's *first wife*!" repeated Ellen, gazing at her with the utmost surprize: "I did not know; I never heard that my Lord had been married before." "Indeed, then," said Mrs. Bayfield, colouring, and looking vexed, "I am sure, my Lady, if I had known, or had the least idea my Lord had not mentioned it, I would never have breathed a word of the matter; but I know my Lord does not like to speak of the late Countess, for her death was so—so—sudden, and shocked my Lord so much, he has hardly ever spoken of her since; and I dare say that was the reason he never told your Ladyship he had been married before."

Ellen, not altogether satisfied with this explanation, still felt somewhat hurt at St. Aubyn's extraordinary reserve: she asked Mrs. Bayfield several questions; such as whether the late Countess was handsome; who she was before her marriage; how long she had lived after it; where she died—and to all which Mrs. Bayfield answered with some appearance of reserve, and as if she felt impatient to dismiss the subject; that she was very handsome and very young when my Lord married her; that she was a distant relation of his own; and that all the family were anxious for the match; that they were married about three years; had only one child, a son, who had died at a few months old, and that the Lady had died abroad. "And what was the cause of her death, Mrs. Bayfield?" "Indeed, Madam, I do not exactly know," answered Mrs. Bayfield, looking a little confused: "she died, as I have told your Ladyship, abroad, and suddenly."

Ellen said no more, for she was above the meanness of attempting to learn from a servant what her Lord apparently meant to conceal from her knowledge; yet she felt even a painful degree of curiosity to learn some farther particulars of her predecessor, whose early death she thought must have caused that gloom of countenance and manner which sometimes even yet appeared in St. Aubyn.

The boudoir within was fitted up in the same style as the drawing-room, but with rather more simplicity, and contained a light bookcase, with gilded wires, and some elegant stands for flowers, &c. Mrs. Bayfield seemed so anxious for Ellen to hasten from these apartments, that she took only a cursory survey of them, determined to take a more accurate view of the paintings and ornaments some other time, when she should have learned to go about her own house without a guide. The boudoir being the last of the suite of apartments on that floor, they next ascended the noble staircase, and visited the bed-chambers, &c. and a large saloon filled with specimens of the fine arts: capital pictures, busts, models, &c. here met the eye in every direction, and here St. Aubyn joined them, and dismissing Mrs. Bayfield, took Ellen's arm within his own, and pointed out those objects most worthy of her notice. Charmed with all around her, and delighted with his attention and the perspicuity of his explanations, Ellen felt as if she had gained a new sense within the last few hours, so little idea had she before of the wonders of art, selected by the hand of taste. From this room they went to the library, where they had supped the night before, at the other end of which was a greenhouse, divided from the library by folding doors, filled with the choicest plants and flowering shrubs, and round the walls of which a gilded net-work served as an aviary for some beautiful canary and other birds. This greenhouse, kept constantly warm by concealed stoves, in the midst of winter gave an enchanting prospect of perpetual spring. Beyond the green-house noble hot-houses and conservatories ensured a constant succession of the finest fruits and more tender flowers.

In the library St. Aubyn and his grateful Ellen sat down together, and there he explained to her his wishes as to their manner of living for the next half year: he told her, that undoubtedly she would, for a time, be somewhat engaged with the few neighbouring families who remained in the country for the winter, and whom he expected, of course, to visit her: "But that once over, my love," said he, "let us propose to ourselves some rational mode of happiness, which shall not be dependent on the whim of others; you are so young, and have powers of mind so extensive, that it will be easy to supply those defects in your education which the retired situation in which you lived rendered unavoidable; and this may be done without any parade or *eclat* of any kind, as it is by no means unusual for ladies to take lessons by way of finishing, even at a more advanced age than your's; drawing and music-masters shall therefore be engaged to attend you, if you do not object to this disposition of a part of your time. In French, I will myself be your instructor, and we will mutually improve each other, my love, by reading together those authors you have so long desired to be acquainted with. If you wish to take a few lessons in dancing, that may be done in the spring, when we are in London, and they may perhaps be desirable to give you a little more confidence in yourself; for, in my eye, no acquired action, or fashionable attitude whatever, could compensate for the loss of one simple natural grace, already so conspicuous in my sweet Ellen: and as to dancing, I am so strange a being, that I cannot bear the idea of a married woman's ever exhibiting herself in public, and being exposed to the impertinent whispers and hateful familiarity of a set of coxcombs." "I wonder," thought Ellen, "whether the former Lady St. Aubyn was fond of dancing." "In the spring, then," continued St. Aubyn, "we will go to London for a month or two, just to see a few of its gaieties, and if I can prevail on Lady Juliana Mordaunt, a very stiff, haughty old aunt of mine, to forgive the dereliction she fancies I have made from my consequence, by marrying, as she supposes, below me, she will be your best guide and most respectable chaperon." "Ah," sighed Ellen to herself, "what shall I do with these stiff proud people: I wish I had remained what I supposed myself, plain Mrs. Mordaunt."

A slight trace of anxiety passed over her countenance, which St. Aubyn perceiving, for in quickness of apprehension and ready penetration no one ever exceeded him, he said:—

"Fear nothing, my love; I am by far too happy, and too proud of my choice, to pay the least attention to the suggestions of either Lady Juliana or any other person: if they come forward handsomely, and as they ought to do, they shall be indulged in the happiness of visiting you; if not, never will I, or shall you, make the slightest concession to them. I will have you support your dignity, even your pride, if pride be necessary, and look down with contempt on such insignificant beings. There is one family near us, Sir William Cecil's, where I hope we shall be very intimate: he is a widower, and has three daughters: the eldest, Laura, from a disappointment in the early part of her life, has remained single, and is now I suppose nearly thirty: the second, Agatha, is married to Lord Delamore, and is gone to live in Scotland: the youngest, Juliet, is still a child, and has bad health: she is a most amiable creature, and has extraordinary talents, but is so unfortunately delicate that she scarcely passes a day in tolerable health. Laura Cecil devotes herself to her entirely, scarcely ever leaving her: she has superintended the whole of her education, as she did that of Lady Delamore, who is some years younger than herself, and to whom Laura was most tenderly attached. Agatha was eminently beautiful, and Laura is a handsome woman, with a great deal of dignity in her air; yet without hauteur of affectation. I hope you will be on very friendly terms with her." "Indeed, my Lord, from your account of Miss Cecil," replied Ellen, "I most sincerely wish it. Next summer, I hope, we shall go into Wales, and then perhaps you will permit Joanna to return with me." "Of that we will talk hereafter," said St. Aubyn, rising hastily. "Let but the spring pass over and all be well, and my Ellen's wishes shall be my law; but beyond the spring, at present, *I dare not look*." "And may I not yet inquire——"

"Ask not, inquire not," interrupted St. Aubyn: "let me, if possible, forget the dreadful, the hateful subject.—And lives that being!" he exclaimed, in an agitation which mocked restraint—"lives that being who has the power to shake the soul of St. Aubyn; whose vindictive pursuit may yet deprive me of——"

He stopt: his pale countenance was instantly flushed to scarlet, and he hastily left the room; while Ellen, amazed, confounded, seemed as if every faculty were suspended; yet in ten minutes this mysterious man returned to her, composed, and even cheerful, neither his countenance nor manner bearing any traces of the emotion which had so lately shaken his frame: he solicited Ellen, as if nothing extraordinary had passed, to ring for her hat and pelesse, and to go with him into the pleasure-grounds. She readily complied, and was, if possible, more surprised and delighted by the grandeur and beauty of the shrubberies, gardens, &c. than she had been with the interior of her magnificent abode.

END OF VOL. I.

[1] It is probable most of my readers have heard the little pathetic tale here alluded to, and which Mr. Spencer has told very sweetly in his little poem, entitled Beth-gelert. For the advantage of those who have not met with it, we insert the following account:

The tradition says, that Llewelyn the Great had a house at the place now called Beth-gelert, and that being once from home, a wolf entered it. On Llewelyn's return, his favourite greyhound, Gelert, came to meet him, wagging his tail, but covered with blood. The prince was much alarmed, and on entering the house, found the cradle of his infant overturned, and the floor stained with blood. Imagining the dog had killed the child, he instantly drew his sword, and killed the greyhound; but turning up the cradle, found the babe asleep, and the wolf dead by its side. Llewelyn deeply repented his rage, and built a tomb over his ill-fated greyhound. Mr. Spencer has thus beautifully described the event:

The hound all o'er was smear'd with gore,
His lips, his fangs, ran blood!
Llewelyn gazed with fierce surprize,
Unused such looks to meet:
His fav'rite check'd his joyful guise,
And crouch'd and lick'd his feet.
Onward in haste Llewelyn pass'd—

O'erturn'd his infant's bed he found,
With blood-stained covert rent!
And all around the walls and ground
With recent blood besprent!
He called his child, no voice replied;
He search'd with terror wild;
Blood, blood, he found on every side,
But no where found his child.

Llewelyn then passionately accuses and kills the greyhound.

Aroused by Gelert's dying yell,
Some slumbers waken'd nigh;

What words the parent's joy could tell,
To hear his infant's cry!

Conceal'd beneath a tumbled heap,
His hurried search had miss'd;
All glowing from his rosy sleep,
The cherub boy he kiss'd.

No scratch had he, nor harm, nor dread;
But the same couch beneath,
Lay a gaunt wolf, all torn and dead,
Tremendous still in death.

Ah! what was then Llewelyn's pain?
For then the truth was clear,
His gallant hound the wolf had slain,
To save Llewelyn's heir.

Vain, vain, was all Llewelyn's woe:
"Best of thy kind, adieu!
The frantic blow which laid the low,
This heart shall ever rue."

[2] See Lettres d'une Peruvienne.